FROSTY PROXIMITY

A GRUMPY X SUNSHINE NOVELLA

WINTER WANDERLUST
BOOK 2

LIZ ALDEN

ALSO BY LIZ ALDEN

<u>The Love and Wanderlust Series</u>

The Night in Lover's Bay (free prequel short story)

The Fling in Panama

The Slow Burn in Polynesia

The Second Chance in the Mediterranean

The Rival in South Africa (standalone novella)

The Player in New Zealand

The Best Friend in Indonesia (free standalone short story)

<u>Aged Like Fine Wine Series</u>

Rosé with My Fake Fiancé

Riesling with My Roommate

Prosecco with My Professor

Cava with My Colleague

<u>Winter Wanderlust Series</u>

Nutcracker with Benefits

Frosty Proximity

Ghost of Ex-mas Past

<u>Wanderlust Resort Series</u>

Beach Boss (free standalone short story)

Beach Resolution

Put it in Beach Mode

<u>Standalones</u>

The Boudoir Arrangement

To the people who love gooey, warm holiday stories that bang.
Hallmark with an O-face.

1

KARA

THE NICEST HOTEL ROOM IN BASEL, SWITZERLAND, HAS A VIEW of the Rhine River, a tastefully decorated sitting room with Louis XV furniture, and a minibar.

A minibar that my friend and client, Clara, just told me to avail myself of.

"Bea?" I call toward the en suite bathroom, where my other friend is unpacking toiletries.

"Yeah?"

"Clara said to help ourselves to the bar." I open the mini-fridge and peer in. Someone has removed and replaced some of the tiny bottles of liquor with full-sized champagne bottles. I pull out the first one and hold it up. "Do we want to open the expensive bottle of champagne?" I reach for the next one and read the label. "The really expensive bottle of cham-pagne? Or . . . " I set the two condensing bottles on the wet bar counter and pull out the third. "The really, *really* expen-sive bottle of champagne?"

Bea emerges from the bedroom and looks at the bottles before raising an eyebrow at me. "Nice try, but you are out of order." She reorders the three bottles. "Least to most," she says, pointing.

"My question still stands."

She points to the middle one. "This is Clara's favorite. Nash took her to the Champagne region last year for a tasting, and that was the winner." Clara's boyfriend is constantly taking her on amazing foodie trips. Even though I've known him longer than I've known Clara, there was never any spark between us, so I can be super happy for the two of them and only a smidge jealous because I want that with someone one day.

"Can you taste the difference between two brands of bubbly?"

"Nope."

I pluck up the least expensive bottle. Bea grabs glasses, and soon, we've got two flutes of sparkling gold liquid in hand and are toasting each other.

"To the best clients in the world," I say, raising my glass.

"To the best boss in the world," Bea returns. We clink and sip, both of us letting out a sigh.

Sure, this isn't *our* hotel suite, but we're getting to enjoy it. Clara's boyfriend, Nash, is Bea's boss and my client. The two of them are attending a gala tonight. We're here to help them —Bea to handle them during the event and me to get them ready for it.

I've been a personal stylist for Nash for years, ever since his career at Heartly, a social media company based on an algorithm that promotes positive vibes, took off and put him in the spotlight. He's brilliant, but like most utterly brilliant men, he was clueless in the style department.

Enter me, Kara Dobreva, stylist extraordinaire.

When we first started working together, it was a wardrobe refresh—or, well, a wardrobe *creation* because I advised him to get rid of most of his stuff—and event-based styling. When Bea came on as his assistant, we quickly became friends. She is the one I work with to choose attire appropriate for his schedule, coordinate appointments for manicures, waxes, and fittings, and keep up with the latest trends, especially when he's attending a public event with photographers.

Like this gala tonight. It's for some charity with a mission I can't recall, but Nash and Clara's outfits hang in the bedroom's closet, pressed and fitted. My hair and makeup kits are in the bathroom, and the only things missing are Clara and Nash.

"What time do they get here again?" I ask.

Bea grins. "Are you wondering how long we have this suite to ourselves? They'll be here in about an hour and a half."

I slump onto the couch in the sitting room next to Bea. "This is the life. Can you believe we're getting paid to be here?"

Bea laughs and crosses her legs, resting an elbow on the back of the couch. She's already dressed for the event in all black, designed to fade into the background while Nash networks and, one hopes, has a good time. We both sip, and then Bea asks, "What are your Christmas plans? Headed back home, right?"

"Well, tomorrow I have the fitting day with Peter before he goes to observe Hanukkah with his family. So, I won't be leaving as early as the rest of you." Instead, I'll be spending the morning having Peter try on clothes I've purchased for him as his personal shopper.

"Oh, right. You've been working with Peter since February?"

Peter is Heartly's European equivalent of Nash. They're both programmers who have advanced to management, although the office in Zurich that Peter works at is much smaller than their New York office.

"Yeah. We did two virtual wardrobe edits, where I cleared out a ton of his stuff, organized outfits, and ordered new clothes. This will be the first time we'll work together in person."

Bea squints. "Do you enjoy working with him? Any time I talk to him on the phone, it's very . . ."

"Grunty?" I supply.

"Professional," she corrects. "I know him and Nash are friends, but Peter has never been all that friendly to me."

When I first met Peter virtually, he'd been a referral from Nash, and when we'd spoken over the phone, he'd been open to a thorough makeover.

I'd done my research and knew how he dressed. Nash had been your typical tech bro, and Peter was, too, but with a European twist. Clients send me pictures of styles they like and want to emulate, and I use that as a guide to develop their personal style. I'd also given him resources and verbiage to use when he went to the salon.

I sigh. "He's hard to get a read on. I think he looks great, but does he agree?"

"I'm sure he does. You are so good at your job," Bea assures me. "The manscaping alone was a vast improvement."

Telling a guy to wax his unibrow isn't rocket science. That's what my family would remind me, which has some extra sting because my sister Daria is, literally, a rocket scientist.

Bea sits up. "Where's all his stuff?" She looks around as if an entire collection of clothes is hiding in this suite. It's big, but it's not *that* big.

"It's in my room with Nash and Clara's luggage for their trip to the Alps."

"If you have the same room I do, yours must be full."

"I'm just glad hoop skirts aren't in style. A single one would take up half my closet. But even if they were, Clara wouldn't wear them." I loved dressing Clara because she was all about the classics. The Jackie O of our generation, without the politics.

Bea relaxes back down on the couch. Her champagne flute is almost empty.

"Enough about my plans. What about you?"

Her southern drawl is charming as she responds. "What would really be 'the life' is getting to stay here for the holidays. What I wouldn't give to be joining Nash and Clara in the Alps."

"Hang on." I mirror Bea's pose, propping my chin up on my hand. "You'd rather spend the holiday with your boss and his adoptive family, which includes *his* boss, in a strange place instead of being with your family? I would say that I relate to this so hard, except your family is amazing."

"My family *and* my ex."

I groan. "Oh my god. I forgot that his family is besties with your family. You have to see him every year?"

"Yup. See, a Swiss chalet with my boss and his family sounds better than my Christmas plans."

"Which are?"

"Tomorrow morning, I fly back to New York and drive to the same Podunk town we go to every year and rent a cabin big enough for our family *plus* his. And if I dare complain, then I get reminded that we never should have dated in the first place."

"Oof."

"Oof, is right. Hence the need for libations," she says, raising her glass.

Bea and I drink our champagne and poke around the hotel room. The best part is definitely the view. When we first got here, the bellhop who helped with our bags—there were a lot of them on account of all the clothes—pointed out that if we angled ourselves just right and looked down the Rhine River, we could see France on the left side and Germany on the right.

Even though it's December 21st, there's no snow on the ground. Being in a cozy Swiss hotel in winter without snow on the ground is like being in France and not eating a baguette or being in New York and not going to the Statue of Liberty—which, in true New Yorker fashion, I've never done —and the forecast says that a ton of snow will arrive on Christmas Eve, but by then it'll be too late.

I'll be back home in the Bronx with my parents and three sisters, probably sitting in the living room of our apartment, drinking hot cider and listening to them play *Agricola*, an annoying strategy game that my family loves to play.

Neither Bea nor I top up our drinks, and an hour or so later, when Clara and Nash arrive, it's a flurry of activity, wishing each other Merry Christmas and exchanging warm hugs.

"Kara!" Clara exclaims, wrapping her arms around me.

I respond in the same tone in the way we've done for years. "Clara!"

She looks like a winter princess with her faux-fur lined duster I picked out for her last year and cheeks rosy from the cold. Clara sheds the coat quickly in the warm room and takes off the matching hat, revealing dirty blonde hair that's compressed against her scalp. She needs a shower—they both probably do—before I style her hair.

"Hey, Kara," Nash says, pulling me in for a sideways hug. "Merry early Christmas."

Nash is tall and lean, with warm brown skin from his Arabic parents, just a few shades darker than my olive tones. His Roman nose and thick, wavy hair make him more serious than he is. Nash is a complete goner for Clara and has been for years.

The hotel room door is still open, and Peter Toch steps into the room.

Seeing Peter for the first time in person is a combination of *wow, that man is serious* and *damn, I'm good at my job*. He's wearing an outfit I put together for him, and now that I can see him in real life, little details stand out that I hadn't noticed before, like how soft his hair is and how dark his eyes are.

The most striking thing about Peter is his jawline. When I first met with him virtually, one recommendation I made was to trim his facial hair back to stubble and show it off. It could cut glass—a nice stylist pun since he has a diamond-shaped face.

I squee a little inside, thinking about how I get to touch him over the next twenty-four hours.

In a totally professional sense, of course.

Peter is my *client*. Anything else would be inappropriate.

And, keeping with my *totally appropriate thoughts,* I offer him my hand. "Peter, great to meet in person."

"Hello, Kara. It's good to see you." Peter is soft-spoken, with a mild accent. After talking with him, I had done a bunch of furious Googling since I knew nothing about Switzerland beyond cheese, chocolate, and banks.

He shakes my hand, his eyes serious, taking in the room. Peter lives in Zurich, which is an hour away, so I wonder if he's ever stayed in Basel before. He's got his own room, and when I tell him that his suit is there, he just nods again and then leaves while I'm distracted by a question from Clara.

I hope I'll at least get to see him dressed before they leave.

Clara and I slip into our easy routine that we've perfected over many galas and charity dinners: she showers, washing her hair, and emerges from the bathroom in a robe to beckon me in. I blow dry, style, paint, and then help her wriggle into her dress and make sure she has whatever undergarments she needs. I have a stash of sheer tights if it's going to be too cold, pasties if she's worried about a nip slip, bobby pins, safety pins, nail polish, deodorant . . . anything Clara might need.

Of course, she doesn't carry it. Bea does.

Nash dresses in an all-black suit with hunter-green accents. It is a Christmas-themed event, and Clara's dress is the same hunter-green with accents of white.

It's nostalgic for me to chat with Clara while we talk about her flight here. She used to fly in for an event from exotic destinations, and I'd hear about months of adventures.

Last year, around this time, Clara backed off on her traveling and moved in with Nash, turning her focus more toward inner-city experiences instead of globetrotting. Her blog, *Worth Going,* is now the platform she uses to explore the diaspora of New York. My parents, who emigrated our family to the US in the 1980s, even helped her out once, introducing her to some of the Bulgarian community in the city.

"How are your parents?" I ask after I've heard all about the flight connection in Paris.

"Good. Dad and Uncle D say hello and ask if you are *sure* you don't want to crash our family Christmas?"

I laugh. Clara's two dads—Craig and Rolf, whom Clara calls Uncle D—know how much being the black sheep of my family pains me. But if I didn't come home for Christmas, I'd never hear the end of it.

"I'm sure. Besides, I may have to deal with my family, but that's better than being the seventh wheel at a romantic Swiss chalet."

Clara makes a face. "My niblings will be there."

I give a rogue lock of hair a teasing tug before I pin it back into place. "I wish I could. Molly, Ricky, and Benny are way more well-behaved than my sisters' kids."

"Ah yes, the Dobreva grandchild hoard."

Clara's wry look makes me grin. My parents love being grandparents. But us Dobreva girls were always driven to excel at school and achieve the best in our careers, not necessarily to be the best parents, and my niblings are . . . a lot.

For my sisters, who have jobs at Lockheed Martin, Google, and Heartly, they rely a lot on my parents to babysit, and my parents spoil their grandchildren rotten.

Yup, my youngest sister, Tanya, works for Nash's

company. That's how I got the job styling him, and she never lets me forget it.

"Trips like these are great because if I'm not in the city, I can't babysit. Guess whose 'flexible schedule' and 'frivolous job' have her being voluntold to babysit?"

I put a safety pin in my mouth and nudge Clara's arm up. She obediently raises it while I see if I can get the fabric tucked in a little further to get rid of a weird shadow at her hip.

When my mouth is free again, I finish my thought. "Kids are the worst."

Clara glances over her shoulder at me, but something behind me catches her eye. "Well, well. Look how nicely Peter cleans up."

2

—————

PETER

As if I needed yet another reason my crush on Kara needed to fuck off and die.

I wonder if all of her single clients interested in women have crushes on her because she makes me feel like the sexiest man alive every time I talk to her.

Like right now. Kara looks me over from head to toe. She's doing her job, studying me and looking for flaws in the outfit she picked out, but then she glances back up and smiles so wide it lights up the room.

"You make that suit look amazing," she says. "The color brings out the gorgeous shades of gold in your eyes, and it shows off your shoulders. And that haircut still looks perfect."

She says these kinds of compliments to everyone, I know, but they still make me feel like my heart is melting anyway. I've heard her compliment Clara and Nash, too, always centering the compliments on something positive about our bodies.

"I wasn't sure if you would have time to style the hair," I say, gesturing at myself.

"Of course," she says. "Let me finish with Clara, and I'll be right with you."

I walk out of the doorway to the bathroom that I've been lurking in and retreat to the sitting room. Nash and Bea are sitting on the couch, reviewing notes for the event tonight. Nash looks up and gestures me over, asking me a question about one of the attendees tonight. I take a seat in one of the upholstered chairs next to the couch.

Nash and I didn't used to work so closely together, but since Rolf, CEO of Heartly, has retired, we're both taking more of a forward-facing role. Tonight, for example, is a publicity event for Heartly's Coding Young program. Nash and I are both passionate about getting kids coding as early as possible. My family encouraged me as soon as I could read, and Rolf encouraged Nash. We used to compete against each other in Heartly's codeathons, and, despite my reluctance to socialize, Nash is one of the few people at Heartly I would call a friend.

"Peter."

I glance up from the attendee list. Kara approaches with some pomade in one hand.

"Can I?" She gestures at my hair.

"Yes."

"Good, stay right there."

I stay still as Kara stands in front of me.

"Sit up."

I do, straightening my spine.

She nudges my knee with hers, and I make room for her between my legs.

"This height works well and is probably more comfortable than the edge of the tub." She digs her fingers into whatever is in the container and sets it on the low table, rubbing the product between her hands.

I close my eyes and let Kara work. She runs her hands through my hair and moves my chin with the dry back of her hand as necessary. She talks as she works, murmuring cute little directions at my hair like "yes, you go this way" and "behave" and "right there."

It's endearing. That crush that formed after a few video chats blooms somewhere deep inside of me, but I tamp it down. There are plenty of reasons I shouldn't be attracted to her: I'm her client; she lives in New York; she's passionate about fashion and appearances, and I'm so inept and careless at that stuff that I *need* her to help me.

And she doesn't like kids.

But my body does not get the memo, even with my eyes closed. Kara's fingers push my hair around, dragging against my scalp and sending jolts of heat down my spine. At first, we aren't touching anywhere else, but then she shifts a little closer, and her leg knocks against my hand.

I move it. Neither of us acknowledges it. Just one more example of how this is Kara's job, and there's no reason for her to apologize for being in my personal space.

I don't apologize because it would be a lie.

She's warm, and I want to grasp her calves and wrap my fingers around the back of her knees. Who would have thought that was an erotic place?

So erotic my dick is interested too.

The back of the elbow has an unsexy name in English, something that rhymes with *penis*.

Wenus. Maybe the back of the knee has an equally unsexy name too.

Wenus. Wenus.

My mother's wenus.

There. Erection problem solved.

Just in time, because Kara swipes her thumbs over my eyebrows, which get unruly, and declares her work done.

I open my eyes as she steps back.

Kara picks up the tub and screws the lid on, moving over to the corner where she stashed her bags.

Clara stands behind Nash, studying me, her head tilted. "Your hair looks great."

"Danke."

When Clara and I first met six months ago at a company event, she peppered me with questions about living in Zurich and the travel I've done until Nash swooped in. "Honey, when Peter gets to one-word answers, his battery is getting low. You've probably used up half his battery yourself. Leave some juice in there for the rest of us." They avoided me for the rest of the evening, which meant I could lurk in the background until I was ready to talk again.

"Nash," Clara says, directing my attention to my colleague. "Are you ready to go?"

Bea straightens the papers in front of them and closes the black leather folder and answers for all of us. "All ready."

"Kara," Clara calls toward the bathroom, where our stylist disappeared. "Do you need us to do anything out here to clean up?"

Kara emerges with a plastic case that looks like a toolbox.

"Nope. I'll take care of all this. Enjoy your evening and raise lots of money for. . .the kids? Right?"

Bea stands. "Yup, the kids this time."

Right. Kids. Kara doesn't like kids.

I love kids. Someday, I want kids of my own. I'm thirty-two, and so far, I can't find a woman who wants to settle down and have babies with me, but that doesn't mean I've given up on it.

Even though my sister's kids are growing up so fast. Sylvie is fifteen, and Noah is ten. Any dream of them growing up with my kids is now impossible.

But still.

"I've got your business cards in my clutch," Clara tells Kara.

"Thanks, but I doubt there are going to be that many potential clients there. I don't travel across the pond for just anyone." Kara grins at us and winks. "You're the exception. But if a New Yorker compliments you, please pass it along."

"Deal," Clara says.

I open the door for Clara and Bea to pass. Nash stops before leaving the room. "You don't have too much to do, right? You should go have some fun tonight."

Kara reaches behind me to grab the door, and I step out of her way. "I have to get ready for Peter's appointment tomorrow. But I'll have dinner out."

"Good. We won't see you tomorrow before we leave for Chamonix. Merry Christmas, Kara."

I mumble Merry Christmas while Bea and Clara sing the words.

In the elevator, Bea folds her hands in front of her and catches my eye. "You know, Kara is quiet when she's working with you."

"Oh, that's true," Clara interjects. "She always talks my ear off when she styles me. Lots of 'girl chat.'" Clara wiggles her shoulders when she says it.

"Kara talked to me." Didn't she?

Bea tilts her head. "She talked to your hair. Or your eyebrows. It's cute. But it's not the same as when she styles Nash or Clara."

I don't say anything. Has my demeanor discouraged Kara from being herself around me? Or does she dial it back for some other reason, like she's trying to be professional? She's friends with Nash and Clara, but we don't know each other well enough to be friendly.

"By the way," Nash speaks up. "I'm sure Kara was going to arrange a driver to get to the airport tomorrow, but since you'll be working with her, maybe you could just take her? It would be a nice thing to do."

"Of course."

"Good," Nash nods. "And before I forget, thanks for missing your family time tonight. I know being with them for the menorah lighting is important to you, and I do feel bad since we usually divide the holidays between the two of us."

I wave Nash's concern away. We've had this discussion many times over the years, but this is the first time that Christmas and Hanukkah overlap. Today is the third night of Hanukkah, and Christmas is just a few days away.

"This is important." My family understands how special this program is to me, and the event planners who organize it are right; people give more during the holidays. Families like Nash and Clara's—wealthy ones who are jetting off for Christmas—will use our party as their last work obligation before they take a break to be with loved ones.

"Will you make it tomorrow?"

"Yes."

"Good. Stick with us tonight. Clara will chat anyone's ear off who steps near you so you can save your energy for tomorrow."

As an extrovert in a company full of programmers and tech people, Nash is used to dealing with introverts. I just have to get this over with before I can rejoin my family.

I make it through the car ride and into the event for an hour or so before I break down and step outside the room. It's eight p.m. anyway, and my family has already lit the candles and recited the blessings.

I dial my mother's number, and she answers on the second ring, speaking in Swiss-German. "Peter, shalom. How is the party?"

"It's fine."

"Did you find a balcony? Or are you in the lobby?" Her voice has a slight tease to it. My mother knows me too well.

"Empty ballroom next door," I say.

"An empty ballroom this close to the holidays?"

"Yeah."

"Have you raised a lot of money?"

"I'm not sure. They don't keep a running tally."

"Did you bid on anything in the silent auction?"

"Of course. You should hope that I win. You and Papi can take an anniversary cruise."

"It's your money; you should go on the cruise. Bring someone special."

There's a moment of silence, and my mother hesitates. "Is there anyone special?"

"No," I assure her. "It'll just be us for the holidays."

"If you are seeing someone, you should bring them by," she's quick to add.

"I know. But after last year . . . it's just better if it's us. Only family."

"Okay." Her voice is tinged with sadness. It's been a tough few years for our family, and guilt tugs at me every time I think about how I was responsible for ruining our family's Hanukkah celebrations last year.

I should have known better.

"How is Sylvie?" I ask.

Mami sighs. "She's a teenager."

Of course, that's an understatement. My niece feels misunderstood, angry, bullied . . .

I just hope that this year will be better than the last.

"Have you seen the weather reports?" Mami changes the subject to what's being called "the storm of the century."

"Yes, it looks like it'll be nasty. I'm glad it will be further north. And I'll be at your place tomorrow, long before the snow hits."

"Good, good. Well, get back to your party, go bid outrageously on something because it's for a good cause and you're far richer than you need to be." Mami chuckles.

My mom, who won't let me buy her a new house, likes to tease me about how much money I make.

We say goodbye and hang up, and I head back to the party. I know it's good work and an important cause, but I'd rather be with my family.

3

KARA

AT NINE A.M., I KNOCK ON PETER'S DOOR. HE ALSO HAS A SUITE in the hotel, albeit one that looks down on the city instead of on the river.

Last night, I tidied up Clara and Nash's room before getting a recommendation from the concierge for dinner. I had a lovely meal on a heated sidewalk overlooking the Rhine. I've been keeping an eye on the weather and this nasty storm that's rolling through north of us, but it looks like it'll be coming in far enough away and late enough that it won't interfere with my flight.

Today, I'm focused on Peter's wardrobe fitting. As a stylist, I offer a lot of services to my clients, and this is one I don't get to do very often. Digital wardrobe edits got popular during Covid, where I would have a three-hour video chat with someone and help them clean their closet out and organize outfits. We talk about the articles of clothing, and I get a feel for how my client likes to dress. What pieces fit them well, what they like about them, how they put outfits together.

I did this almost a year ago with Peter. Today, our goal is

to provide him with some new outfits to supplement the work we did previously.

Peter opens the door dressed casually in tan pants and a polo.

"Good morning," he says.

Peter is a man of few words. I learned quickly that he's not interested in chit-chat or frivolous conversation, so I rein myself in around him.

"Good morning," I return, stepping into his room while he holds the door open for me.

In the corner of the sitting room is one of the hotel's luggage carts filled with hanging bags. Some of the clothing I ordered in advance, but some I purchased from shops the day before yesterday. Basel has some fine clothing stores, especially on Freie Strasse.

"Ready to get started?" I approach the rack and begin unzipping bags, looking for the first outfit I want him to try on. When I'd asked Peter via email how the clothes I'd picked out for him last time were working out, he'd sent me an itemized list. It required a bit of translating.

Red sweater - too tight

Translation: the Burgundy cable-knit, merino-wool-cashmere sweater didn't fit well enough for his tastes.

Blue pants, the ones with the two buttons - wear often

Translation: the navy, fitted stretch chinos that he'd been skeptical on had passed whatever test he'd put them through.

And so on.

I was surprised that so many of the clothes he "wore frequently" were some of the more unconventional items I'd suggested: brighter colors, patterns, unusual fabrics.

I've leaned into that with this visit, so I hope it's the right way to go.

We go from casual to formal, starting with some warm, cozy pieces that make me want to sink my fingers into them while Peter wears them.

I don't, obviously. That would be weird.

Then we move through business casual, and I get to ask fun questions like "How does it feel in the crotch?" and "Is the inseam okay?" which is just a professional way of asking how his junk feels.

Next is the business formal. Peter had commented that some of the jackets were getting a little tight around the shoulders, so I've got a collection of new suits to try. When he comes out with a tailored pale gray suit on, I check the seams on the shoulders and press gently to feel where they fall on his body.

I'm not sure what Peter does to have this build. Swimming? He's got such a nice, tapered frame, and these pants make his butt look amazing.

I snap my head up, mentally slapping my cheek. *Stop staring at his butt. Be a professional.*

I step back to look at the length, the cuffs, the color, and tap my chin. "Hm. This outfit needs something."

Peter looks down at himself, holding his hands out to the side. He waits.

I glance back at the rack of clothes, and my eye catches on a small box from a local shop here. The eye-catching display in the window had lured me in, and I was delighted to step into the millinery.

"I got it," I tell him and retrieve the box. When I lift the hat up, Peter eyes it with skepticism.

"It does not look practical. Or warm."

"Not everything has to be practical. There will be a time and a place for this hat."

He is unmoved, so I pull out my tablet and swipe through some photos. "Look, here's Lewis Hamilton wearing one just like it. And," I swipe through a few more photos to find a photoshoot from Vanity Fair, "here's Alwin from Verduistering wearing it in plaid."

"Okay." Peter nods. That's about as enthusiastic as he gets, so I'll roll with it.

He reaches into the box and pulls the hat out. It's a hunting cap, soft and slouchy with a short bill. It has a silk lining, and the top is made of gray wool, just one shade darker than his suit and softer than it looks.

Peter puts it on and turns to face me. The fit is good. I lift it a bit to sweep his unstyled hair back underneath it and then nod once. "There. Go take a look."

He returns to the bedroom, where there's a full-length mirror, and I put the lid back on the box. He looks great in the hat, so I'm pretty confident I can get him to keep it. "What do you think?" I call.

Peter doesn't answer, so I pause, listening. Not hearing anything, I walk to the open door and peer inside.

Standing at the mirror, Peter stares at himself. My stomach falls. Maybe he hates it. Have I misread him so poorly?

Just when I'm about to suggest he take it off, the most bizarre thing happens. Peter's lips tip up, his mouth opens, and his lips stretch in an actual, hand-to-god smile.

Now, Peter doesn't just look good in the hat; he looks *devastating*. It's downright magical. A Christmas miracle.

Our eyes catch in the mirror. Peter's always given off an air of amusement when he finds something funny, but honestly, it's not like I've been meeting him at comedy clubs or watching romcoms together. I know he likes Nash and Clara, but seeing him in person with them last night hit home how serious Peter is.

His corporate headshot doesn't even contain a smile.

I've been quiet for too long, and things have gotten awkward. The smile's gone, and I clap my hands together once for lack of anything better to do. "Well, okay. You like it, I guess?"

"Yes."

"Right. So, ready for the next suit?"

He nods and reaches for the button of the jacket. I force myself to back out of the doorway and grab the next suit—the last one—and bring it to Peter.

He's unbuttoning the shirt at the wrists when I return, and my mind immediately plays the imagination game and envisions him rolling up the sleeves, revealing muscular forearms and light skin.

I take the jacket and flee, closing the door behind me. I remind myself that he's a client. I'm a professional. Just because he's got an amazing body and a sexy glower does not mean that I can afford to be interested in him.

When the door opens again, I'm composed, and we decide to keep this suit too. Peter changes back into something casual while I sort the clothes into what I'm sending with Peter and what needs to be returned.

"What time is your flight?" Peter asks from the doorway. The outfit he chose to wear is his favorite chinos and a new wool sweater, a little bigger in the shoulders now, and dark teal.

"Two p.m. I have to pack up some things here but you can go whenever you're ready."

"I will drive you to the airport."

I blink at him. "Are you sure? It's going to be an hour or so before I'm done."

Peter checks his watch. "Yes. Nash asked me to, and I have time."

"Oh. Okay."

Peter walks over to the couch, where a messenger bag waits. He pulls out a laptop and opens it on the small desk in the sitting room.

I turn my attention back to packing and eventually call hotel staff to come in and take some of the clothes away to be sent back to the store or mailed. I work quickly since Peter is waiting, and I'm done in forty-five minutes.

"All done. These need to go to your car," I tell him. "I'm

going back to my room to grab my bag and then I'll meet you downstairs?"

He nods, and we split up.

On the way to my room, I pull out my phone to check my notifications. There are two missed calls from my sister, Daria, which is weird.

As soon as I escape the elevator, I call her back.

"Hey," she says as soon as she answers. "I'm desperate. Can you please come by and take Bella to daycare? I'm running late, and apparently, there's a meeting with the higher-ups that I need to sit in even though I—"

I cut her off. "I'm in Switzerland."

"What?"

"I'm in Switzerland," I repeat. That familiar irritation prickles my chest. "I mentioned it in the group chat that I would be out of town for a few days."

"Why are you on vacation? Aren't you coming to Christmas?"

"I am," I say with more patience than I feel. "I'll be back tomorrow. And I'm not on vacation; I'm working with clients."

She laughs a little. "Working with clients? A client flew you to Europe?" The laughter in her voice is now incredulous.

"Yes." I bite my cheek as I use my keycard to enter my hotel room.

"Oh my god, I don't want to tell rich people how to spend their money, but wow, to be that spoiled is wild."

The last thing I want to get into a discussion about right now with my sister is the ethics of working in an industry entirely reliant on disposable income while still believing that capitalism sucks. Instead, I get back to the original point. "So, you'll have to figure out something else to do with Bella."

"Oh, Kara." My sister sighs. "Don't be mad at me. I just

forgot. You know, with my postpartum depression and going back to work, life has been a little hectic around here."

My sister knows how to immediately soften me and make me feel bad for her despite the fact that there's always some excuse for forgetting about my life. She's not wrong—she has been struggling, and I do what I can to help, but this time she's out of luck.

She hangs up shortly after, still in search of child transportation, and I get to packing.

When I exit the front door of the hotel five minutes later, Peter is in his car, a dark Volkswagen sedan idling by the curb directly under the three flags jutting from the hotel's facade. The street parking here is weird: there's no curb, but instead, there are posts that divide the parking area from the street, and a minor change in the texture of the ground signifies the pedestrian area.

There's also EINFAHRT painted onto the sidewalk, which made me giggle.

Peter helps me load my bags, and then it's a ten-minute drive to the Basel-Mulhouse-Freiburg airport—named after the three closest cities in Switzerland, France, and Germany, respectively—and located in France. Yes, residents of Basel drive to another country to fly. We don't talk, but I steal glances at him when I'm not watching out the window.

Growing up in New York, I never learned how to drive. Usually when I'm in a car, I'm always on my phone, but here —maybe it's because the car, the driver, and the view are all foreign—I pay more attention.

The roads around us have a steady stream, lots of cars but not really traffic. Peter drives confidently, navigating roundabouts and merging lanes, which are all intimidating to me. Plus, I can't read any of the signs—thank goodness for the ubiquitous airplane icon.

We cross the border into France—still very much in the

city—and my phone dings in my bag. I dig it out and check my messages.

UNKNOWN NUMBER

Dear passenger, unfortunately, your flight has been canceled. Please log in to our website to manage your booking. We apologize for the regrettable inconvenience.

"Oh crap."

Peter glances over at me.

"My flight's been canceled. Hang on, let me look to see what's going on."

"Should I stop?"

I can see the airport. "No, keep going. I'll rebook my ticket, so we might as well just get me to the airport."

I pull up the airline's website. There, in a bold red banner across the top, it says:

"The following airports have been closed due to inclement weather:"

There's a whole list of airports, including mine.

"Inclement weather? What inclement weather?" I say to no one. The sky is . . . well, it's gray, but that's not surprising. The temperature is even milder than normal. I navigate to my weather app and select my location as Basel.

Things get ugly.

"Um, Peter?"

He glances over at me.

"The storm's moving faster than they predicted. It's going to hit tonight."

4

PETER

"Have you tried looking for a different airline? Or a flight out of—"

Kara cuts me off with a raised hand, brow furrowing as she stares down at her phone and resumes typing with both thumbs.

This must be one of those situations where it's just better if I keep my mouth shut. Kara's a grown woman, running her own business, which involves travel a lot. Surely, she knows how to figure this out.

But has she ever been to Switzerland before? She may not realize how small the country is or what other airports there are.

As happens so often, I don't have enough information to be useful, so I say nothing.

"Okay," Kara interrupts my train of thought and looks up. "Can you take me to the train station? I can use that to get to Zurich, and there's a flight to New York in three hours."

I check the time. The Zurich airport is twenty minutes past my parents' house in Baden. Depending on traffic, I should be able to get Kara to the airport and still be at their place by sunset to light the menorah.

"I'll drive you," I say, putting the car back in gear and checking the traffic for an opening to pull out onto the street.

"The train is fine, Peter. It might even be faster."

I shake my head and depress the accelerator, speeding up to get behind a small silver Škoda. "You'll have to wait at the train station here and wait again at the transfer."

"But it's so far out of your way."

"No. I am going to Baden."

Out of the corner of my eye, I see Kara consult her phone again. "Oh," she mutters. "That's close to Zurich."

"Yes."

"Are you sure?"

"Yes."

That settles it. Kara leans back in her seat and watches out the window as we cross back into Switzerland and drive through Basel again.

"Is that where your family is? Baden?"

"Yes."

More silence.

"Who are you spending the holiday with?"

I tense. My family has been a difficult subject lately. "My parents, my sister and her family. My grandmother."

"No girlfriend?"

"No." Why is she asking? If I was dating someone, they would have come with me last night if we were serious. And if we weren't, she wouldn't be coming to celebrate with my family.

"Sounds small and quiet. My family is big and loud. I'm one of four, you know?"

She doesn't expect a response, which is good because I didn't know. Was I supposed to?

"And two of my sisters have kids. Four of them so far, all under five years old." Kara presses the nail of her thumb to her other fingers one by one, making her first knuckle turn white from the pressure.

Maybe she's nervous about getting home. While I don't spend every night of Hanukkah with my family, it's hard to imagine going without the ritual of the lighting of the menorah, the baking of challah, frying sufganiyot, and having wine by the fireplace at least once over the holiday. And Christmas is a much bigger time for Americans than Hanukkah is for us.

The best thing I can do for her is get her to the airport. The only thing I can think of to say is, "Don't worry, I will get you there."

Kara watches the view out the window, over the Rhine again and out of the city the other way. The last thing we talked about was Kara's sibling's kids, but I know she doesn't like kids, so I'm unsure if she wants to talk about them.

After a few more minutes of silence that even I know is uncomfortable, I suggest I put on a podcast. I put on an episode I'm halfway through about accessibility and user interface.

"—and we have to remember that the UI experience and building an accessible web application depends on more than using ARIA roles and accessible labels—"

After a few minutes, Kara's phone dings, and she lifts it up. She doesn't lower it for a while, and she's not typing but swiping. The screen is angled slightly away from me, so I can't tell what she's doing. Maybe reading?

After we pass my parents' town, we hit traffic. There are tunnels leading into Zurich, and with holiday traffic and the incoming storm, it's clogged. I catch Kara glancing at me a few times and realize my knee is bouncing in the footwell.

I wish for the traffic to clear so I can get Kara to her flight and drive to my parents in time for the menorah lighting.

It finally does move again, and within ten minutes, I'm pulling up at the curb of the departures area. It's crowded, but in the normal way of a busy airport and not in the stalled way of travelers piling up with nowhere to go. It's still open. We made it in time.

Kara grabs a luggage cart, and I help her with her bags. Once her things are out, I close the trunk and offer her my hand. "Thank you, Kara. Have a merry Christmas."

She clasps my hand. "My pleasure. Enjoy the holidays with your family."

I watch Kara disappear into the airport with a sinking feeling in my gut that I don't understand. As I pull away from the curb, I put the podcast back on and try to pay attention.

I pass the end of the runway, where a wind sock swings lazily. See? It's not even windy yet. It's cloudy, but there's no snow.

She'll be fine.

The podcast host says something about CSS scripts, and I realize I haven't caught a single word since I left the airport.

I hit the pause button and ask my phone to read me out my new messages. The robotic voice confirms that I have many: group chats with my family, a message from Nash saying it was great to see me and wishing me a happy Hanukkah, and then text messages from my mother.

The automated voice reads her messages in a deadpan, of course, but I hear them pitching as only a mother's can:

"Peter, I wanted to remind you to bring the book for your father. I don't know if you'll have time to run home."

"You're probably driving right now, but I just ran into Mr. Abernathy. His daughter is single again."

"You should have been here by now. Are you okay?"

I tell my phone to call my mom, and she answers on the first ring.

"Peter! Where are you?"

"I had to swing by the airport. It's a long story, but I'll be there in ten minutes."

"The airport?"

"I was dropping a colleague off."

"Someone flying out? If their flight hasn't been canceled yet, it's going to be."

"How do you know?"

"The storm is coming in too fast. I swear, these meteorologists are just guessing."

I sigh.

"Whoever you dropped off should go back home before they get stranded."

"They—Mami, the person I dropped off was flying home."

"Can they take the train?"

"Flying home to the States," I correct. "*She* is flying home to the States." And then I sigh again because this is not going to go well.

"A colleague? Or a friend? You know what, never mind. You have to go back and get her."

"Mami, I can't. This is supposed to be our family only."

Mami scoffs. "You can't leave her alone. They'll close the airport, and this storm is going to snow us in for days. She'll be alone for the holidays. Is she Jewish?"

"I don't think so."

"Well, never mind. We can't close our doors to her."

"Are you sure about this? Even with—"

"Yes." Mami's voice is firm. "If she's a transphobe, then we'll lock her in a closet or something with a dreidel and slip her Linzers under the door. At least she'll be safe and warm and technically not alone."

That makes me laugh. "You can give her a reading light and your annotated copy of *The Transgender Teen*."

"With a fifty-question quiz she has to score perfectly on before she can come out and join us."

"All right," I concede. "I'm turning around. Warn everyone, okay?"

"I will. And Peter? It's going to be okay."

With my mother's words ringing in my head, I take the next exit and circle back toward the airport.

5

KARA

THERE'S A MASSIVE LINE OF PEOPLE BECAUSE, *OF COURSE*, THERE is. I wonder if everyone in Switzerland is trying to fly out of Zurich because the line snakes around and around. I have my bags on a cart, the garment bags draped on top, and I join the line.

I pull out my phone and gladly update Clara and Bea in the group chat. They'd texted me while I was in the car with Peter.

BEA

> Just boarding my second flight. Heathrow was a mess—I'm guessing it's this storm? Kara, are you at the airport?

> And Clara, didn't I make you swear to send me pictures of the chalet? You have to tell me how awesome of a job I did picking it out.

> Unless you hate it.

> Then it's all Nash's fault.

Since I'm waiting in line, I open the chat and look at the photos again. There's the chalet from the outside, snow in

33

fluffy white piles around the sides. Another picture of a roaring fireplace with an e-reader and two pairs of legs, which I'm guessing belong to Nash and Clara. One out in the snow of Ricky and Molly building a snowman. Molly's mouth is open in a shriek, and Ricky's finger is up his nose.

KARA

Made it to Zurich's airport. Line is hella long, so I'm crossing my fingers that I'm going to make it.

CLARA

We are crossing our fingers for you.

Haha, I just made my whole family cross their fingers and wish for you to make your flight home.

It's a sweet gesture. And making the flight to get home and be with my family for Christmas is going to be great.
Right?

BEA

I'm almost to the cabin. It feels like I have to push through the air to get there. I swear, my ex misuses the laws of nature to make it difficult for me to make progress.

CLARA

Like matching magnet poles?

BEA

Exactly.

Please send me more pictures of your vacation so I can be insanely jealous of the warm and fuzzy vibes.

Clara sends more photos. It's Rolf and Craig holding a tray of cookies and wearing aprons that have mustaches on them and say, *Mr. Right*. Then there's another one with a cozy fireplace and a big Christmas tree, which looks like something that belongs on a Hallmark card. And lastly, there's Nash with a mug in hand, a whipped cream mustache over his real one, wearing a T-shirt that says, *!false: it's funny cause it's true*.

I'm glad Clara is having a dream Christmas.

Or maybe it's not that lovely. Just because the photos are beautiful doesn't mean the actual vibes are too. Rolf and Nash are probably talking about work too much, and maybe Clara's niblings are behaving like mine—i.e., lots of screaming and running and making a goddamn mess out of everything.

The line inches forward, and I send—less enthusiastically—a message to my family's group chat.

KARA

I'm at the airport. Lots of lines, so I hope I can make it through security on time.

NEV

Hope so. I'm ready to kick your ass at Risk 2210.

Nev is my older sister who works for Google. My youngest sister, Tanya, the one who works for Heartly, sends a picture of her two kids. They've got what could be either flour, powdered sugar, or cocaine on their faces. Since my sister is staunchly anti-drug, I doubt it's cocaine, so odds are pretty good it's powdered sugar going on the snowball cookies my mom is baking.

Man, those kids are going to be so hopped up by the time I get there. They'll probably have a sugar rush hangover tomorrow.

Which my mom will treat with a Christmas-themed hair-of-the-dog breakfast serving French toast.

There's a collective groan in the line, and then voices are raised, and people get antsier.

Oh no.

I check my email, and yup. This flight has been canceled.

Son of a bitch.

No one is moving from the line, and the email says to please see a staff member to make arrangements. I have nothing better to do, so it looks like I'll be spending Christmas snowed in an airline-budget hotel in a foreign city.

I hope the hotel has room service. And a bathrobe and tub. That doesn't sound so bad, actually. I could watch TV until the power goes out and then switch to one of the shows I have downloaded on my tablet. I'll rewatch *Single All the Way* and *Elf* without having to listen to kids in the background or explain to them why everything Jennifer Coolidge does is funny. Maybe I can run to a store and buy hot cocoa packets.

It may not be a Swiss chalet, like Clara's family, but it'll be cozy and quiet . . . and lonely.

Or, knowing my luck so far, they'll be out of hotel rooms, and I'll have to bunk at the airport.

I shift on my feet and switch to the Heartly app and scroll through some photos. I need the good vibes right now while I wait to determine my fate.

The line moves up; some people—probably locals—leave instead of waiting. I don't have that luxury, so I lean on my cart and keep scrolling.

Until I hear a voice calling my name.

"Kara!"

I straighten up, looking around until I see a familiar flop of hair. "Peter?"

I'm halfway through the line, so there are layers of people between me and Peter, but I see him pop up over some heads as I stretch on my toes at the same time he does.

The crowd parts as he weaves his way to me in the goddamn middle of everyone.

"What are you doing here?" I ask when he arrives.

"Your flight is canceled, yes?"

"Yeah . . . "

"Come stay with my family. We're not celebrating Christmas, but it's better than being alone. And safer."

"I . . . " I didn't think that Peter would make this offer, so I'm too surprised to answer right away. I glance at the line in front of me. Do I want to crash Peter's family Hanukkah, or do I want to wait in line on the off chance that I'll be able to get a hotel room?

"Please," he says, and that's what does me in. Staying with strangers and one guy I barely know might be crazy, and as much as a quiet Christmas alone sounds amazing, it does sound lonely too.

"Okay," I agree.

Peter nods and takes the cart from me. Navigating out of the center of the line is a mess, but Peter is insistent and polite, throwing out a "Fro'i Fiirtig!" to everyone as they let us pass.

Soon, we're outside, making our way through the parking lot to Peter's car. Once again, we reload all of my stuff back into the trunk, and Peter slams the hatch.

When the car turns on, that same damn podcast is back, the one that I'm pretty sure my sisters listen to and talk about all the time. It's so smart.

I love my family, but I've always been the black sheep. First, there were spelling bees and science projects and hackathons while I was excelling in art classes and preferred watching *Queer Eye for the Straight Guy* instead of playing deep strategy games like *Gaia Project* or *Power Grid*.

My family called me a sore loser.

And maybe I was at the games. But podcasts and news articles led to discussions that led to me being quiet in the corner, not something I am naturally inclined to be. As I got older, my version of acting out was making friends and being outgoing enough that even when my family isolated me, I always had somewhere else to go.

Now here I am, in a car with Peter, listening to the exact same shit. Peter is so like my siblings sometimes, it's disturbing. I wonder what he would say if he knew that I had to retake Calculus in high school or that I didn't finish college, not even for fashion or design.

That's always been a bone of contention in my family, something that's brought up every time we're together. If I'd just *applied myself*, my parents like to say, then I would have done better.

I bet Peter's family asks me those getting-to-know-you questions, and I'll have to admit that I'm not smart enough or too lazy for college. Peter's family is probably all super smart too. They might also be quiet like him. I might be zooming at fifty kilometers per hour toward a few days of dreary silence while a storm locks us inside.

I slump down in my seat.

When we get back onto the highway, Peter reaches over and turns off the podcast. He's focused on the road, which is good, except that his knuckles are white as he grips the steering wheel. I didn't notice that before when he was driving me to the airport. Is it the upcoming storm that has him so tense?

Peter said his family lives close by, so I am sure we will get there before the storm hits.

Though it is definitely a lot grayer outside.

Peter's frowning too. Sure, he's normally a pretty serious person, but this is a deep frown.

And he keeps glancing at me.

Peter flexes his hands, releasing the death grip, and taps his fingers on the steering wheel. He glances at me again and shifts in his seat.

I cross my arms and wait.

We exit the freeway underneath the sign for Baden. Once there's an opportunity, Peter pulls over to the side, puts the car in park, and faces me. Or, faces me as much as he can with his seatbelt on.

"Listen, my family . . . " He stops and rubs the stubble on his jaw. "My sister will be there with her husband and two kids."

"Okay," I drawl.

"You don't like kids, I know."

I hold up a hand before he can continue. "I'm great with kids most of the time. I can behave myself, I swear."

He shifts again, and I wait for more.

"My niece," Peter says, pushing the words out. He's staring at me, gauging my reaction. "She's fifteen and going through a tough time. I know kids get moody and hormonal at that age, but you should know that she's trans too. And if you have a problem with that—"

"Whoa, whoa," I stop him, both hands up now. "I have no problem with that at all. Come on, would Nash work with me if I was a bigot?"

"Some people don't allow their bigotry to show until they find an opportunity to hurt someone."

Peter's words come out with an overlay of pain and bitter truth. I swallow back any further protests. I know I'm lucky to be in an industry where being different is more celebrated than normal, and I'm surrounded by people who are generally pretty accepting. Heck, even my sisters, who I don't see eye-to-eye with often, are involved in Diversity, Equity, and Inclusion programs in their respective companies.

I could tell Peter about all the people in my life who are under the LGBTQIA+ umbrella, about how one of my favorite neighbors is a drag queen, or that love is love is love, but I know that it would just be words. "I look forward to meeting your family," I say instead.

He nods, and the crease between perfectly plucked thick eyebrows and the set of his stubbled jaw tell me that he's still anxious about it, but that will fade with time and trust.

And Peter is trusting me with his family, even before considering his niece. *All* of his family.

"I've never attended a Hanukkah celebration before."

Peter's hands relax a bit. "We're more secular than traditional. My dad was raised in France as a reform Jew. The community here is Orthodox."

A few minutes later, we pull to a driveway next to a small structure, and Peter turns off the car. Silently, we gather as much of our luggage as we can carry, and Peter leads me to the door of the building.

There's a window to the left with a single electric menorah on the sill.

"Hello," Peter calls as he opens the door. There's a staircase leading down, and I realize this house is on the hillside, and we've parked at the top.

I brace myself for the rushing of feet and voices of greeting, but all is quiet except for a woman who calls from below, answering in Swiss-German.

Peter responds, gesturing for me to leave my bags by the door, and I follow him down two flights of stairs.

We enter a kitchen, which is cozy and white, and there's an older woman bending over and peering into the oven. His mother, I guess. She and Peter converse for a minute before she straightens up and wraps him in a hug.

When she pulls back, they're still talking in Swiss-German, her eyes flicking back and forth from him to me. Her face is open and warm, as opposed to Peter, who looks nervous and is trying not to show it.

"Kara, this is my mother, Nora. Mami, this is Kara."

Nora offers her hand for a shake, which I take.

"Thank you for having me. I know it's a big inconvenience over the holidays to house a stranger."

Peter's mom puts her hands on her hips. She's much shorter than Peter and soft, with graying blonde hair and reading glasses on her nose. She peers over them at me.

"Well, you agreed to come here even though there are plenty of hotels in Baden. We can always toss you into one of them if we need to." A quick smile and a twinkle in her eye tells me she's kidding. "We're happy to have you."

Her tone changes to instructional, but they are in Swiss-German. I expect it's something like "show her to her room," but then Peter responds, and there's some back and forth. Next thing I know, Peter's turning around and heading out the door, I assume to get the rest of the luggage.

"Come on," his mom says. "Let's get your bags downstairs."

I follow her back to my luggage. She mutters something under her breath and then says to me, "You don't travel light."

"It was a work trip," I explain. I grab the garment bags before glancing out the window in time to see Peter pull away from the curb. "Wait. Where's he going?"

She grabs my carry-on bag and tromps down the stairs. "To pick up his grandmother."

Okay then. I'm alone with his mother.

It takes a few trips, but we get my luggage down the stairs and into the guest room. The bottom floor is small, barely a hallway with two closed doors, the bedroom I'm staying in, and an open door through which I can see a sink and toilet.

"Get settled in," Nora says to me. "I'll be in the kitchen. Let me know if you need anything. It's not a hotel, but hopefully, it'll do."

I stand in the room after she leaves, looking around. There's a bed with a striped duvet on it and two pillows. It's not a single, but it's not a queen, either.

The space is a little utilitarian—definitely a guest room— but there are photos on the walls, which I wander over to look at. There are a few photos of Peter, one of him in a suit I picked out for him with his mom on his arm and a stiff smile on his face. Then him, even younger, in various family configurations, including a photo of the whole family—Nora and an older gentleman who must be Peter's dad, a woman with short hair and a sensible outfit who has the same eyes and must be his sister, a man with olive skin next to her, and the two kids, one an infant in their dad's arms, and the other about five with dark hair wearing shorts and a T-shirt.

Everyone's dressed casually and smiling happily—well, I guess what passes for happily with Peter.

There aren't any more recent pictures of the kids or Peter, so I open the closet door and peek inside. It's empty save for a few boxes, so I hang the garment bags up and tuck the stuff I won't need over the next few days into the closet and out of the way.

Noises drift up from downstairs, the soft thumps of cabinets opening and closing and the water running: Nora working in the kitchen.

I sit on the bed and pull out my phone.

KARA

So . . . I'm at Peter's parents' house . . .

CLARA

Oh no! Did your flight get canceled?

Kara

Yeah.

What do you know about his family?

CLARA

Not much. I met his mom once. What's their house like?

KARA

Modest. No one's here except for his mom, so it's oddly quiet.

BEA

Wow, so you're going to spend
Christmas/Hanukkah with Peter and his
family?

KARA

I guess so.

Peter's mom seems nice. She's teased me
already, which is so different. You know how
he is.

BEA

Like talking to a rock sometimes? A very
smart rock? Yes, we know how Peter is, lol.

CLARA

But we also know how you are. You'll win
them over.

I send a heart emoji and put my phone on the nightstand.

An extra loud clang comes from downstairs. I take the stairs back down and join Nora in the kitchen. It's a narrow space, with cabinets above the counter that close the kitchen off from the small dining area. Aside from the table with six chairs, there's a wall of built-in shelves covered with books that immediately catches my eye.

Before I can wander over and look at titles, though, Nora pauses chopping vegetables to offer me wine.

"Red or white?" she asks.

"I'll have whatever you're having."

She retrieves two wine glasses from the cabinet between us and pops the cork out of a bottle sitting on the counter. It's red, deep and lovely in color.

Nora sets a glass in front of me and lifts hers. "Proscht."

I clink my glass to hers. Nora takes a sip and then gets back to chopping.

"Where is everyone else?"

"My husband, Liam, is helping the neighbor wrap their

pipes. My daughter and her family are shopping for some last-minute supplies. They should be back soon."

I nod. "That makes sense."

The air fills with the *snick, snick, snick* of her knife.

"You're American," she says, glancing up and taking in my features. "Where are you from?"

"I live with my parents in the Bronx. But they emigrated from Bulgaria when my older sister was a baby."

"How do you know my son, then?"

I take a fortifying sip of my wine before answering. "I'm a personal stylist, and Peter hired me."

The knife stops moving, and Nora stares at me. "*You're* the stylist?"

"Uh . . . yes?" What did I do to deserve that reaction?

"Huh," is the only response I get before Peter's mom resumes chopping. If she was going to say anything else, though, she doesn't have the chance because the front door opens and voices ring out that are not Peter's.

Nora drops the knife and intercepts the newcomers at the bottom of the stairs. I turn on the stool, watching as Nora grips a young boy in a tight hug. She squeezes his face before she puts a hand on the back of his head and propels him toward me.

I smile and wave. He's about ten and has that same dark hair the kid in the picture had, but he's too young. He must have been the baby in the picture. He's followed by a teenager, and this must be the niece Peter was worried about. She's tall and thin, with slightly lighter hair than the rest of them have. They politely introduce themselves to me as Noah and Sylvie. Noah bounces away while Sylvie drifts toward one of the chairs and tucks a foot under her butt.

Nora gives a brief hug to the woman who must be Peter's sister, but the woman catches sight of me and gives me a huge smile.

"You must be Kara," she says. "I'm Juna, Peter's sister. It's so nice to meet you. Are you a hugger?" She holds her arms out, and I stand from the stool to accept it. "I've heard so much about you."

That surprises me. "You've heard good things, I hope?"

"Well," she says as I settle back on the stool, "I've heard enough to know who you are and that you are good at your job. But I'm also surprised you are here."

I sip my wine, and she leans in.

"Are you sleeping with my brother?"

I choke on my wine, blowing some of it over Juna and some of it into the bowl of my wine glass and getting back-splash right in my face.

6

PETER

WHEN I WALK IN THE DOOR WITH MY GRANDMOTHER, IT SOUNDS like a party is happening. I was hesitant to leave Kara here with my mother, but Mami had made a good point: Grosi couldn't stay alone for days while the storm rolled through. She lived close enough that my sister was going to pick her up and drop her off on her way in every day, but we were bracing for the worst, and that meant Grosi was coming to stay.

I had helped her pack some things she needed and grabbed as many of the emergency supplies that I could find in her house—more flashlights and blankets than necessary, honestly. It was a good thing there were four bedrooms in the house.

Grosi was in her nineties, and her memory was not the best. She'd said grandsons twice on the trip over, and I had to gently correct her every time. I ignored the *great-grandchildren* part and just focused on her not misgendering my niece. Hopefully, no matter what Grosi said, it wouldn't be as bad of a Hanukkah as last year.

But that was up to Kara, wasn't it?

"Grosi is here," I call out. But no one hears me. I guide Grandmother down the stairs and into the kitchen.

Noah is the first to notice us. He's a good kid, into football, just like his mom. At ten years old, he looks a lot like I did—lanky, nose slightly too big for his face, hair that does whatever it wants.

He gives Grosi a quick hug, and then I wrap him up in a bear hug, growling. He squirms away from me, laughing.

I scan the room, looking past Mami and Sylvie in the kitchen and Papi and Tom, my sister's husband, pouring themselves glasses of scotch and generally getting in Mami's way, and spot Kara. She and my sister are looking over the bookshelf together, animatedly talking about each book they pull out.

It's Mami's bookshelf, but Juna's read most of them. She and Kara are in the romance section, filled with old-school paperbacks. Most are in English, but some are German translations.

Kara looks up and catches me watching her. The smile she gives me is slow and tentative, but based on the nearly empty glass of wine and the flush of her cheeks, she's already having a good time with my family.

After introducing Grosi to Kara, I leave her with Mami at the kitchen island. I wrap my arms around Sylvie, who also squirms away from me but less successfully than her brother.

"Uncle Peter, you just saw me last week," she complains.

"So?" I kiss the top of her head and let her go. She hurries to smooth her hair back, but she's smiling too. I leave her alone and walk toward my sister and Kara.

"Well," Juna says, straightening up from the bookshelf and waving me over. "Look who you dropped into our family." She speaks in English for Kara's benefit.

Juna is athletic and a middling height, fitting right under my chin when I hug her. She's the one that got the coordination and athleticism in our family. Her hair is cut short, not stylish enough to be a pixie but sensible enough to keep up with her busy lifestyle.

"I know it's not ideal," I say in Swiss-German. "The airport—"

My sister waves me off. It's not that she isn't concerned for her daughter—she is—but she's eternally optimistic, the person who believes the best in everyone. "There's always room for more. Besides, she has *great* taste in books."

My eyes widen. I know the kind of books my sister reads, and they aren't our mother's romance novels.

Kara's cheeks flush a little darker, and mine heat too. Last I heard, my sister was reading alien romances, and they were . . . *creative.*

"Go away." My sister pushes me. "I'm stealing her." She loops her arm through Kara's and turns them both back to the bookshelf. "Now, have you read this one?" I hear as I walk away. "Because he's got horns that function as a handlebar."

I get a drink, greet the rest of the family, and pour myself a glass of wine. There's not much left in the bottle, so I take the rest and refill Kara's glass. The two women are unsettlingly quiet while I do it.

Mami's sliding dinner into the oven, and I know we'll be lighting the menorah soon. Normally, we would light it at sunset, but the sun had set while I was picking up Grandmother, so we've missed that window. I remember that my bags are still in my car, my arms too full with Kara's stuff and then Grosi's, so I leave the wine on the counter and rush back out to the car to get my bags. The snow is just starting to fall, and the wind is picking it up and swirling it in white tornadoes on the street. Other houses in the neighborhood are lit with Christmas decorations, while ours has a soft glow from the menorah in the window.

I wipe my shoes on the rug at the door before removing them and descending the stairs, the sounds of my family's merriment rising. I take a left to my usual room and come to a halt just inside the door. Kara's things are in here; her suitcase is against the wall, unzipped and flipped open to show a collection of shoes and a bulging plastic bag, the kind hotels offer for laundry services. Her phone is on the nightstand and her messenger bag is on the bed.

I back out quickly and duck into the next room. There are bags in here too: from the looks of it, my sister's and her husband's.

There's only one bedroom left, and my shoulders slump. That one is going to be Grosi's.

I set my bag down at the top of the stairs and descend. The family has moved to the back room, the one with the big windows looking out into the backyard with the iron stove. Tom is getting the fire going, which will probably be maintained for the next few days. We've got plenty of firewood to last us through the storm and more out back.

In the center of the back window is the real menorah. It's not lit yet, so I approach Mami.

"What did you plan for sleeping arrangements?" I ask.

She sighs. "Well, I gave Kara the guest room."

"Yes. I saw that."

"And your sister and Mami are going to share one bed."

"They are?"

She shakes her head sadly. "I don't want Mami to wake up confused. You know she's not doing well, so I thought it would be best if one of us stayed with her. And then Sylvie is going to sleep on the floor of my room."

"So then, who's sleeping in Juna's old room?"

"Tom and Noah."

"Mami. Where am I sleeping?"

"You have a choice. You can sleep on the couch in the front room or on the floor in Kara's room. Or, you can share the bed with her. She's your friend, after all."

"She's not my friend, she's . . ."

Mami tilts her head. "If she's not your friend, then why did you invite her?"

"Are you mad at me because I did?"

"No, but it is an awfully nice thing to do for someone you don't like."

I cross my arms. "You're putting words into my mouth. I never said I didn't like her."

"So, you do like her?"

"Well, yes. She's nice and—"

Mami pats my cheek. "Couch or share the room with her, your choice." She turns to the rest of the room. "Are we ready?"

7

KARA

"Have you celebrated Hanukkah before?" Juna asks me as we gather around the menorah. There are five candles in it, one in the center and four on the right. She stands just to the left of it, me next to her, and Peter to my right. The rest of the family fills in the circle around, ending with Noah.

"No," I say. "I know the general story about how the oil miraculously burned for eight days, but that's it."

"First, Noah will light the middle candle, the shamash, and then we recite the blessings. You don't have to, but if you want to say amen at the end, you can. Then he'll use the shamash to light the others on the menorah."

Juna turns to her son. "Chömer?"

He nods and stands before the menorah. When his mouth opens, song comes out. It's sweet and soft, the high pitch of a boy. "Baruch Atah Adonai Eloheinu Melech Ha'olam, asher kidshanu b'mitzvotav v'tzivanu l'hadlik ner shel Hanukkah."

Noah pauses, and everyone says, "Amen." He draws a breath and glances at his mother before continuing. "Baruch Atah Adonai Eloheinu Melech Ha'olam, she'asah nisim l'avoteinu, b'yamim haheim bazman hazeh."

There's another chorus of "amen."

Carefully, he picks the middle candle out of the menorah and guides it to the closest unlit candle. One by one, he lights the four and then places the shamash back in its place.

"Good job," his mom calls, and Noah ducks his head, the classic kids' "aw-shucks."

Peter speaks next to me. "Normally, we spend time together afterward, opening presents, cooking, trying to avoid technology, but since we are starting late tonight, we will eat first."

Nora has already retreated to the kitchen, pulls baking trays and casserole dishes out of the oven, and Juna recruits me to help her set the table. We sit down to eat—a simple roasted chicken and vegetables with latkes fried to a crisp golden brown, and afterward exchange gifts.

Nora is in charge. She passes out gifts wrapped in white glossy paper, and there's even one for me, a small, oval shape she presses into my palm.

"It's nothing personal," she clarifies. "After all, we weren't expecting you. But I won't have anyone in my house going without tonight."

"That is so kind," I tell her. "Thank you." I wish I had a horde of unopened presents to give out, but I did all my shopping back home.

The gifts have a theme—personal care. My oval is a bar of soap, and the fragrance and label need no translation—it's rose.

Peter, sitting next to me, has a travel shaving kit, complete with miniature creams and oils. Across from me, Juna has a bar of soap similar to mine.

I yawn for the fifth time, hiding it behind my hand, but Juna catches my eye. "You've had a long day. Perhaps you should go to bed. You too, Peter."

"Mami," Sylvie says. She asks something in Swiss-German and Juna answers in English.

"We can watch a movie if you and Noah can agree on one."

The kids run off, and Juna grabs my plate while she stands up. "Papi and I are in charge of dishes. You're free to run off to bed. We'll see you in the morning."

I say thank you and good night to everyone, and Peter follows me up the stairs. He grabs a bag next to the banister at the top and starts to walk back down.

"Good night, Kara," he says.

"Wait. Where are you sleeping?" The house is small, and I'm pretty sure there's only one bedroom on the first floor, Nora and Liam's.

"The couch."

"What? No. Peter." I glare at him. "You can't let me kick you out of your own bed."

"Technically, my mother kicked me out of my own bed."

I take two steps down to argue better. "The kids are watching a movie, right? They'll keep you awake. Plus, how comfortable is that couch?"

"What exactly are you suggesting, Kara? Every bed is spoken for. Even the air mattress goes to Sylvie, and she doesn't even get to have any privacy."

"I'll take the couch."

"Then you, who can barely keep your eyes open, have to stay up while my sister's kids watch a movie and have no privacy. I'd rather it be me on the couch."

I swallow. This is what Peter gets for bringing me.

Unbeknownst to him, I would never be able to sleep with the TV on, no matter how tired I was. Especially if it's a movie in English because while I can close my eyes, I can't close my ears.

The opening music for *The Polar Express* comes on downstairs.

"Look," I say. "We're both adults, and it's a . . . well, it's not a queen-sized bed. What do you call them here? Doubles?

Point is, there's room for the two of us. We all have to share a bathroom anyway, so there's a limited amount of privacy. Let's just share for the night and see how it goes."

He studies me for a few moments before answering. "Okay."

"Great." That decided, I turn around and walk back to the bedroom.

Peter follows me, putting his bag on the floor just inside the door. "Do you want to use the bathroom first?"

We could go back and forth all night long, being super polite to each other, or we could just set some boundaries. "I'll shower first. You pick which side of the bed you want."

"Okay."

I pull out the big bag of dirty laundry from my luggage and prop it up in the corner. That's when I realize that I'm out of clothes.

I mean, it's not that I'm out of clothes, per se, but I did shove my pajamas into the dirty laundry, and they are not near the top when I open the bag.

Pushing the bag aside, I dig through my clean clothes options. Nice blouses, underwire bras, a few thongs, and some dressy pants. Work attire, because the outfits I wore casually on my own time are in the dirty pile.

"Um," I start, turning to Peter. "Could I do some laundry?"

He's sitting on the bed playing with his phone, a small pile of folded clothes next to him.

"And maybe you should shower first."

He puts the phone down on the nightstand and rises to his feet. "I'll show you to the laundry."

I grab my bag and follow Peter downstairs. The movie's on in the TV room, casting flickering lights across the faces of the kids and their dad. In the kitchen, Nora and Juna sit at the counter stools, talking quietly over their wine glasses.

Peter speaks in Swiss-German, gesturing to my laundry bag.

"Oh, of course," Nora says, hopping up. She leads me to the laundry room and waits while I pick out the clothes that can go in without getting ruined or needing special care. It's not much, honestly, some leggings and sports bras and my pajamas. I'm going to need to be stingy, depending on how bad this storm gets.

I make note of the time on the machine when Nora starts it and then grab my e-reader from upstairs. The bathroom door is closed and the shower on, so I guess Peter has taken my advice to shower before me. I go to the back room with the big dark windows and the cozy stove. Liam is in one of the armchairs, reading, and glances up when I come in.

"Just thought I'd read for a bit while I wait for my laundry." I gesture to the chair next to him, and he nods.

"Please," is all he says before he returns to his book, a thick hardcover with an embossed spine.

I try to read, but it's hard to focus. There are the soft noises from the TV and the women in the kitchen, the crackling of the fire. Outside, the snow is still a small flutter of flakes, but the wind has picked up. The yard extends pretty far back, and the wind rustles the trees aggressively.

Back home, it's much more difficult to get quiet reading time. There's always an argument happening between one of us sisters or a kid crawling into my lap.

But this is my first night in the Toch household, so maybe they just haven't released their drama yet.

Instead, I'll just enjoy the nice, quiet, dark night . . .

A throat clears and I jerk awake. Movement catches my gaze from the corner of my eye, and I turn my head. Peter walks into the entrance of the room. He's padding gently on socked feet, his hair dark and damp, wearing a shirt and shorts.

"The shower is free." He says it low and soft, and his dad smiles gently into his book.

"I'm going to wait until the laundry is done to come up to shower. I don't have clean pajamas."

Peter frowns. "You'll have to borrow something. We hang our clothes dry."

"I saw that you have a dryer."

Peter's dad speaks up. "It does not work. It is one of those things I have needed to replace, but . . . " he trails off with a shrug.

"Oh."

"Come. I'll get you clothes."

In the bedroom, when I catch up, he hands me a shirt and a pair of pants that are probably going to be eight inches too long, but they are warm and thick. "Go shower. I'll get the rack out and hang your laundry when it's done."

By the time I'm out and dressed and have climbed down the stairs, Peter is in the back room by the fireplace, laying my clothes out on large, metal wire racks.

Including my underwear.

"I can get that," I say, snatching the cotton undies from his grip. Wordlessly, he hands me the basket of damp clothes and leaves.

I've never not used a dryer before. Of course, I've always owned clothes that needed special care, but it's going to take my jeans forever to dry like this. I put the last few items out, draping shirts and leggings over individual bars of the rack. There are already two pairs of panties out—my black cotton thongs—and Peter must have hung them.

Ugh. Of course, I didn't wash any of the *nice* underwear. It had to be the comfortable, basic stuff.

But, wait. Wouldn't it be more embarrassing for Peter to see black lace or a G-string?

I sigh at myself. We're both adults making the best of a

situation. I doubt my cotton panties are going to be the straw that breaks the camel's back.

When I get back to the bedroom, Peter is in bed, the lamp by my side of the bed is on and the glow of his phone lights up his face.

"Ready for lights out?" I ask as I crawl under the covers.

"Yes." Peter turns his phone off and puts it on the night-stand, shifting onto his back.

"Thank you for inviting me to spend the holiday with your family." I turn the light off and turn onto my back too.

"You are welcome. I'm sorry you'll miss Christmas with your family."

I shrug in the dark, staring up at the ceiling. "It's exhausting, to be honest. It was a relief to get away for work because my mom has probably been a nightmare this week."

Living with my parents means that I get roped into *everything*. Even though we're not religious, my mom has huge expectations for Christmas, and it's hard to put my foot down when I need to get work done.

"Anyway, I like your family a lot."

"I like them too." He hesitates for a moment. "You were good with the kids."

There's a hint of surprise in his voice, and indignation rises. Sure, Sylvie didn't actually talk to me much, but I had a great time chatting with Noah. What exactly did he think was going to happen? What did he *think* I would do? Something transphobic?

"Of course I'm good with kids," I snap. "You don't have to sound so surprised."

I can feel Peter gathering his thoughts on the other side of the bed. "I thought you didn't like kids."

"Why would you think that?"

"You said 'Kids are the worst' back in Basel."

I search my memories and land on my conversation with Clara back at the hotel. I bite my lip. I do remember that comment. Perhaps my resentment toward my sisters is coloring my thoughts about my niblings. "I did say that. It was a flippant remark that I shouldn't have said. My sisters' kids are at a difficult age and sometimes I feel taken advantage of around them." I walk such a tight rope with my family with regards to the kids and taking care of them.

"I see." There's a pause, and I wonder if that's the end of the conversation. But then he adds, "I want kids of my own someday."

"I do too." Quiet descends and when Peter doesn't say anything else, I turn onto my side, tucking my hands under my chin and closing my eyes.

8

PETER

BEHIND ME, KARA SHIFTS FOR AT LEAST THE TWENTIETH TIME, causing the bed to bounce slightly. I turned away from her shortly after we said goodnight, though I don't usually sleep on my side. I had caught myself glancing over at her twice and decided that we were too close together to sleep on my back.

Kara shifts again, and I raise my head. "Are you okay?"

She sighs. "I'm so sorry. I should have warned you; I'm not a great sleeper. I'm not used to sleeping next to someone, plus these pants . . . "

I sit up, pushing the comforter down and rubbing my eyes. "What's wrong with my pants?"

"I just . . . they're joggers with narrow ankles, but they're also like eight inches too long, and I can't roll them up, so the fabric just bunches around my feet. I'm not used to pants in bed."

"What do you normally wear?"

She's silent, but in the soft glow of the light from the window, I can see her grinning. Maybe I don't want to know.

"I'm not used to pants in bed either," I confess. I'm wearing a similar pair to what I've lent her.

61

Kara sits up, and we both push back to lean against the headboard. "I hate when you are so tired, but you can't sleep for stupid reasons. This happens to me all the time."

"You've had a busy week and a stressful day. Being stuck with strangers would be hard, even when it's not paired with missing out on your family time."

"And the storm of the century."

"And having to share a bed."

"And stupid pants," she adds with a chuckle. Then she gets serious. "Would it be terrible if I took them off? I'm wearing underwear."

My mind immediately goes to the black thongs I laid out on the drying rack, and my throat gets dry.

"You can take your pants off too," she says casually as if it's a totally normal thing to say to your client in the dark, whom you have to share a bed with.

But if it helps us sleep . . .

"Okay," I agree.

We both rustle under the duvet, and there's a thump against the carpet as first my pants and then hers hit the floor.

"Ahhh . . ." Kara settles onto her back. "So much better. Good night, again."

"Good night."

I must fall asleep because a noise wakes me up sometime later. I prop myself up on my hand, facing the room, and listen.

It's the wind howling ferociously.

A soft voice comes from behind me. "This must be the storm."

I look over my shoulder. Kara stands at the window on her side of the bed. She's pulled the curtain back, and an ethereal light radiates in. Her legs are exposed, but the shirt I gave her falls to mid-thigh. Her arms are crossed, and when I meet her gaze, she holds it for a few seconds before turning her attention back outside.

I kick my legs over the side of the bed away from her and stand at the window on my side of the bed. I gently pull the curtain to the side and look out.

It's white. A swirling, dancing vortex that audibly bites at the window, at the house, at the night. The glass shakes in the frame, and I can feel the building sway with the pull of it.

I glance back over at Kara. "Have you been up long?"

She shakes her head, still staring outside. "Just a few minutes. It's wild." She lifts her chin to the storm.

"Have you ever seen a storm like this?"

"A few. Never this early in winter, but sometimes in January or February, we get an absolute dump of snow. I remember having days off of school and the pictures that circulated—snowmen drag queens being built in Hell's Kitchen, people bundling up and snowshoeing in Central Park, the old men throwing snowballs. Once, my parents even broke out their old dzhezve—a copper coffee pot—and made traditional coffee." She pauses for a moment. I'm watching her, but she's watching the storm. "I haven't seen that pot since. They might have given it away." She turns to look at me. "What about you?"

I look outside again rather than meet her gaze. "We had a storm like this a few decades ago. They called it the storm of the century back then too."

"I guess this is how the climate is now."

Movement has me turning to look at her again, and she's reached up and is tugging the curtains closed. When she's done, she mock-shivers and slides back into bed. "Too cold now."

"It is." I'm not particularly cold, but I climb into bed too. The storm continues to howl, but soon, Kara's breathing evens out, and I follow her back to sleep.

———

I wake up again, this time more refreshed. I stretch my legs, burying my face into the pillow and soft, springy hair. My nose grazes tender skin, and warmth radiates from in front of me, the duvet trapping the heat. I pull my arm tighter, dragging the source closer.

A hum vibrates from my hand up, and I open my eyes. I'm wrapped around Kara, her loose, curly hair in my face, her ass pressed against my morning erection, the backs of her bare thighs against the front of mine.

I ease back, raising my arm slowly so as to not wake her. Once I'm clear, I roll away, planting my feet on the floor and rubbing my face. Kara shifts, and I glance back. I've left the duvet pulled back, and her shirt has ridden up, exposing a pair of baby blue cotton panties, one side pulled up a bit higher than the other, against Kara's smooth skin.

Her hand emerges, blindly reaching back, searching for the duvet. I'm letting the cold air in.

I gently grasp the edge and pull it to the top, all the way up to Kara's neck, and tuck her in. She lets out a sweet hum and goes still.

I wait to make sure she's asleep and then stand, tiptoeing into my pants and the socks I left out. I leave Kara to sleep.

Downstairs, my dad is in the back room, drinking coffee and staring out into the snow. The wind isn't quite as bad as it was in the middle of the night, but it's hard to tell what time it is. The light hasn't changed, and I left my phone upstairs.

"Morning," I say, and Papi startles, nearly spilling his coffee on the paperback he's ignoring in his lap.

"Ah, good morning."

"More coffee?" I ask.

"Please."

I take his mug and retreat to the kitchen, starting the coffee maker again. I notice the time—eight a.m., later than I expected.

By the time I get back with two mugs, Papi has resigned himself to watching the snow enough to close his book.

Papi and I have always been the quiet ones in the family. Juna and Mami are always busy with activities and conversation. My sister is outgoing, and added to her athleticism, she was popular. Since I was four years younger than her, I was constantly hearing about how different we were.

I take a seat in the chair next to Papi, and we drink our coffee. It's mesmerizing outside—a total whiteout. The cold radiates from the window, and I get up and push my chair half a meter closer to the stove.

Someone moved the drying racks to the side, and I'm sure Kara's clothes are dry.

One by one, the family filters in. Juna leads Grosi carefully down the stairs, and we place her in one of the chairs in the front room, where it's more comfortable and away from the cold. Bangs come from the kitchen, signaling that Mami is up, setting out bowls for breakfast and corralling us to help ourselves to muesli, yogurt, fruits.

Kara comes in just as I've sat down with my bowl at the table, the joggers back on and pooling around her ankles.

"Boker tov," Mami greets her.

"Good morning," she returns, and soon, she's next to me with a coffee and a bowl of yogurt and fruit.

I don't know if Mami ate, but she's ready to start the day. The counter is lined with ingredients. My sister has used the excuse of playing games with her kids and has retreated to the front room, along with her husband and my dad.

I take the last bite of my muesli, rinse my bowl in the sink, and grab an apron from the pantry. This is the part I enjoy the most over the holidays—baking with my mother.

"That," Kara says, "is adorable."

When I glance up, her eyes are on me. I look down at myself. My mom's aprons are traditional, flowery and feminine, but they do the job.

"My handsome son." Mami pats my cheek. "Kara, we could use your help too. Pick out an apron when you're done eating."

"Sure," Kara says, standing and meandering into the kitchen while she finishes the last few bites.

It's a small kitchen for three people, and I have to be careful not to elbow my mother in the face while I'm opening the pantry to show Kara the aprons as Mami goes for a pot on one of the top shelves.

"What are we making?" Kara selects a red-and-white checkered apron, looping it over her head and tying it around her waist.

"Challah, sourdough, cookies, and sufganiyot."

Kara holds up a finger. "I'm not familiar with that last one."

"Deep fried doughnuts," I explain.

"That comes later," Mami says. "First, the challah dough."

I know what our job is there, so I stand back and let Mami make the dough until the consistency is just right. Then the bowl is turned out onto the floured counter, and Mami leaves me to instruct Kara on kneading while she washes the bowl for the second batch.

Soon, Kara and I each have a blob of dough and are massaging and flipping, massaging and flipping.

"Look what we're making today." Mami thrusts a paper in front of my face while I knead. "Aren't these cute?"

I pull back so I don't go cross-eyed and read. "Stuffed dreidel cookies? Where did you find this?"

"Pinterest, of course. Don't you think Noah will love them? I bought M&Ms to stuff them with."

Kara leans over to peer at the paper too. "Are the dreidels made with sugar cookies?"

"Yes, we'll work on those next."

Once the dough is smooth, we leave it to rise. Mami has us

mix the sugar cookie dough next, and Kara and I work side by side, leaning over the counter using cookie cutters to make Star-of-David-, menorah-, and dreidel-shaped cookies. Mami takes our scraps, rerolls them, and cuts the pieces she needs for the stuffed dreidels.

Then I show Kara how to divide the challah dough into four lumps and roll them out into strands. Mami is at the stove, humming while she stirs the jelly filling for the sufganiyot.

"Top, middle. Top, middle," Kara mutters while braiding. "This reminds me of a star bread I made once, where you layer dough and then slice it and twist the edges. It was Insta-grammable but not that tasty. Okay, how is yours looking so puffy? Did I do something wrong?"

I look down at Kara's loaf. It's a little . . . lean.

"It's fine. Maybe next time, not so tight on the braids, yes?"

I show her how to tuck the end, and our doughy, clammy hands bump when we both reach to tuck the top under too. I let Kara work, and she braids her fingers together, using her forearms to squish the dough into a shorter, fatter loaf.

I swat her hands away. "Don't mess with it too much. It'll be fine."

Kara crosses her arms over her chest and leans her hip against the counter. "Look at you, Mr. Good with His Hands."

My mom chortles, and Kara flushes. "Good with his hands with bread! Not anything else! That's not what I meant."

Juna enters the kitchen, reaching past us to the fridge. "Is Mami making sex jokes already?"

"She didn't make the sex joke," Kara protests.

"Then who made the sex joke?"

"It wasn't a sex joke!"

My sister smirks. "Sure." She retreats back to the front

room with her bottle of juice. I know better than to protest anything with her and Mami.

"Less sex jokes," Mami says, shoving a plastic bin of food coloring into Kara's hands. "More icing."

9

KARA

Who knew baking cookies could be so artistic? They aren't with my family.

Of course, I'm not feeling particularly charitable to them right now because I woke up to an email from my dad forwarding me a marketing newsletter from a local college and commenting that maybe my few college credits could transfer and I could have a bachelor's degree "in no time!"

Peter and I made several colors of icing and decorated the sugar cookies. After reading a few articles for decorating tips, I figured out how to flood and use toothpicks to fix mistakes.

And then I made an ombre dreidel cookie with blue and white icing.

And a Star of David with blue and yellow marbling.

"Goodness, those look good," Nora says while leaning to inspect my work.

"It's fun. I don't typically get to mix bright colors like this."

Peter's cookies next to mine don't look so great. He attempted the marbling but ended up with a green blob in one corner where he overworked the blue and yellow together. His lines are squiggly, and some of the flooding spilled over—okay, *a lot* of the icing spilled over, and I tried not to watch when he used a finger to wipe it off the counter and then sucked the icing off his finger.

He did it a lot.

I ate my fair share of icing, too, and I've got that feeling in my mouth that my teeth are coated in impending cavities.

Nora doesn't remark on Peter's cookies, instead choosing to squeeze his waist and ask, "Did you have fun?"

My parents, who were strict about the course work that "mattered," like math and science, would constantly praise us for creative pursuits. No matter how terribly our art projects came out, or how much of a mess we made, or if we got less than an A, it was fine because my dad would say that those were "just electives."

Peter returns the hug. The three of us gaze at the piles of cookies.

"Perhaps we can eat all mine before Juna sees them?" Peter suggests.

Nora pats her stomach. "I already snuck the two of the worst ones while you weren't looking. No more for me, so you're on your own."

He releases his mom and picks one of the sugar cookies up. It was supposed to be stripes of red and white, but the lines blurred. A flash of . . . mischievousness? Whimsy? Some foreign feeling passes over his face and rolls through my stomach as he holds the cookie up to me. "Kara? Take one for the team?"

"Nope. Nope, nope, nope," I say, backing away and trying not to laugh. "In fact, I'm going to go brush my teeth."

Peter advances, fighting a smile.

"Go pawn that sugar abomination on someone else!" I spin and run for the stairs.

———

IN THE AFTERNOON, WHILE THE STORM STILL RAGES, WE READ until sunset, light the menorah, and say the blessings again.

Peter's grandmother naps. Most of the adults read books. I'm curled up on the couch with an e-reader. Juna and I swapped devices, and after perusing her *varied* and *eyebrow-raising* library, I settled on a Sierra Simone book.

Peter, Tom, and Noah play with a dreidel in the corner, gambling with what Peter tells me is gelt. At some point, Peter shouts "gimel" and raises his fists in victory while Noah groans. Peter sweeps all the gold coins over to his pile and then flings one at me. I peel the gold back and let the Swiss chocolate melt on my tongue.

The fire crackles, and the only thing we can see outside the big glass window is snow piled up several feet.

Sylvie heaves a big sigh. She is draped over the opposite arm of the couch from me.

Ah, to be an angsty teenager where nothing your family does is fun anymore.

She plays with her hair. Her clothes are baggy, which is fine: I like baggy clothes too sometimes. But Sylvie has this air of skulking about, hiding herself. Her face is bare and has been since last night, and that gives me an idea.

I leave the e-reader on the arm of the couch—closed so Sylvie doesn't get curious and read something she shouldn't —and climb the stairs.

When I return to the family room, she barely glances at me. Instead of sitting on the couch, I sit on the floor in front of it, facing the couch, and set my makeup kit on the cushion.

With a few clicks, my favorite pallets and tubes are splayed out, the mirror up. Over my shoulder, I can see Peter watching me.

"That looks like work," he says, but the corner of his mouth tilts up enough that I know he's teasing.

"Do what you'll love, and you'll never work a day in your life," I parry back, taking a cream concealer out and dotting my imperfections with it: a blemish here, a freckle there. When I have a smooth base, I take out a darker color and suck my cheeks in, tracing along my cheekbones.

Sylvie rotates on the couch, lying on her belly and elbows, watching me.

When I'm done with the shadows, I pluck out a few possible highlight colors. I swipe some samples on the back of my hand and offer Sylvie a look.

"Which color looks best with my skin tone?"

Her eyes dart back and forth between my face and my hand. "This one," she says. It's a bit warmer than I normally go, but that's okay. I sweep it under my eyes, on my chin, across my forehead, blending as I go.

When I'm done, I turn and let her inspect my work. "What do you think?"

She's quiet for a moment. "Good."

I turn and inspect myself in the mirror. "Okay, it's got the Sylvie stamp of approval. How about some of the fun stuff, then?" I wave her over, and she sits on the floor next to me. "I like a bit of shimmer on my eyelids. And maybe some lip stain. Here, you pick a color for me."

Most of these colors fit Clara better than me, but it's not like I'll be leaving the house.

Sylvie picks a raspberry color for my lips, and I apply it.

I turn to her for inspection and blow her an exaggerated wink and a kiss. She laughs.

"Do you want a turn?"

Sylvie freezes, and the room is quiet save the pop and crackle of the flames.

"If it's okay with your mom," I say, glancing back at Juna.

"Yes," she says quickly.

Sylvie picks up a pallet of eyeshadow and turns it over. "I don't know how."

"You never watched any TikTok tutorials or anything?"

She shrugs. "Some."

"Well," I say. "I can teach you, or I can do it for you."

She mulls it over for a moment, and then her answer is so quiet I almost miss it. "Can you do it?" She hands me the eyeshadows.

"Yup." I tap her knee. "Sit cross-legged, just like me." She mirrors my pose, and our knees touch. I grab my box of goodies and hoist it over our heads, setting it on the floor next to me since we don't need the mirror at eye level anymore. I angle the case toward myself.

I start with her eyebrows, not plucking but penciling, making them slightly darker than their natural color and using the pencil to build a bit more shape. I talk the whole time, explaining what I'm doing and why. I make a list in my head of what products I can leave behind for her to experiment with.

Between the performers I followed on Instagram and Heartly, my neighbor's panicked last-minute calls needing to borrow something for a show that night, and my trans clients, I was a lot more equipped to help Sylvie than her mom or an online video.

Next, I contour with powders, which will be softer than the creams. I bring out curves on her brow line and eyes. On her face, which is square, I put shadows under her cheekbones and use a warm color corrector and concealer to hide her hair and then soften her jawline. I use more shadows and highlights than I did with mine, but I am careful not to overdo it.

"You have great lips," I tell her. "Very full. You could have inherited your uncle's, which are much more difficult to work with for a feminine look."

Sylvie giggles, and Peter responds from his chair. "It would be hard work to make me look feminine."

"Don't threaten me with a good time," I warn him.

Then her eyes. Soft brown on the eyelashes and light natural colors on the eyelids.

"You can open your eyes now."

Sylvie's gaze meets mine, and I tap my chin. "What about your hair?"

She runs a self-conscious hand through her hair. It's long, more brown than blonde, but there's definitely some dimension to it, but it's lanky, and without a wash and getting an iron out, there are limited options.

I fish a comb out of my box, close it, and get on my knees, waddling around Sylvie to kneel behind her. I run my fingers through her hair first, then the comb, and then my fingers again. If I smooth it down too much, it'll look harsh when I want it to be softer. I gather sections of hair up, leaving them messy, and start a big, loose fishtail braid to the left side of her head.

I dig the elastic out of my hair and use it on hers to end the braid.

Moving to her front, I fluff the braid segments. It's smoother than I'd like, but the braid is a nice touch.

"Okay," I say, heart pounding in my chest. I spin the box and put my hand on the lid, ready to pull out the mirror. "Are you ready to look?"

Eyes big, Sylvie nods. I lift the top and hold my breath.

She studies herself. Tilting her head, she blinks at her reflection, inspecting her cheekbones and then tilting her chin up to look at her jawline. Then she centers herself again and takes a deep breath.

And then her face crumples as she bursts into tears.

"Oh shit." I panic, horrified. "I can take it off. I'm so sorry."

Juna is there in a flash, kneeling next to Sylvie and pulling her close, muttering softly to her in Swiss-German. Sylvie says something to her mom between sobs.

"I am so sorry," I repeat. I get to my feet and grab some tissues from the box, but before I can return to Sylvie, Peter grabs my elbow.

"Kara. Stop."

I bite my lip and face Peter. I expected a tense jaw, eyes filled with anger or hatred for making his niece cry, but instead, there's a softness in his face that I've never seen before.

Sylvie repeats the same sentence again, and I flinch when Peter's hand tightens, but he relaxes it right away.

Peter guides me out of the room and up the stairs to our bedroom. I sit on the bed and tuck my hands under my thighs.

"I thought she would like it. I am so sorry; your family has been so good to me, and I just thought—"

My words are cut off by Peter's mouth on mine. The kiss is perfunctory, perhaps because I've gone utterly still, so surprised by his actions. His lips are firm and warm, a solid press against mine that disappears before I have time to process it.

"Thank you," he says when he pulls away.

"Um . . ."

"She was not upset."

I shoot him a look. A that's-a-load-of-bullshit look.

"Not a *bad* upset," he amends. "A good upset. She said . . . " He swallows, Adam's apple bobbing under that strong jaw of his. "She said she looks like a girl."

Oh. *Oh.*

Peter reaches out and touches my shoulder, giving the muscle a gentle squeeze. His words are soft and emotional. "It was a good thing."

I take my hands out from under my thighs and place my right hand over his. Our gazes meet, and for the first time since it was decided I would stay with his family, Peter's finally relaxed. Those eyebrows I shaped and smoothed two days ago are relaxed, the tightness in the corners of his mouth gone. Peter looks a few years younger without the stress of protecting his family from strangers on his shoulders.

When my gaze wanders back to his eyes from his mouth, there's something else there.

Peter kissed me. It was quick and thankful and spur of the moment, but it still happened. But Peter is my client.

And here, sitting on this bed that we shared last night, and we're going to have to share tonight, it could happen again.

Neither of us moves. We just stare at each other, the warmth of his hand a steady weight on my shoulder through the cotton of my shirt.

His thumb shifts, ever so slightly, across the collar to brush against my bare skin.

There's a knock on the door, and we both jump. Sylvie calls from the hallway. "Kara?"

Whatever weird spell was between us is broken, and Peter straightens, stepping away to open the door.

Under her eyes and her nose, the skin is red from crying, her eye makeup smudged. "I'm sorry, I didn't mean to get upset—"

I stand and cut her off. "Believe me, you aren't the first person who's gotten emotional after seeing a new look."

I change the subject. There have been enough tears. "Would you like me to do some repair work?"

She nods and flashes a smile.

We go back downstairs, and I apply more concealer and fix her eye makeup. Juna sits on the couch this time, not hovering but keeping a watchful eye on her daughter and what I'm doing.

"I have to admit," she says as I swipe some mascara on Sylvie's eyelashes, "I've never been into makeup. Never. Not even when I was a teenager."

"That's not true," Peter says from across the room. "You went goth for a while. We had to listen to Rammstein, and Mami got upset when you forgot to wash your face and stained the pillows."

I glance at Juna. "You were goth?"

She huffs. "I was a teenager. They do weird things."

"Mami *never* wears makeup," Sylvie chimes in. "Not even to our cousin's wedding."

I cap the mascara. "We're done." I reach into my case and pull out a soft, subtle pink lip color. I raise an eyebrow at Sylvie. "What do you think? Is this a good color for your mom?"

Sylvie grins and looks at the selection, pulling out a few brighter colors. Juna makes a face.

"Part of my job is figuring out not just what makes people look good, but what they'd actually wear. It can be more about how they see themselves as opposed to how society wants to see them. After all, we don't want to look like someone else, right?"

"I guess," Sylvie says. "If I was pretty—"

Juna and I both protest, but I get my words out first. "Don't. You're very pretty, and if I have to convince you of how pretty you are, I'm going to say some nice things and make you cry again."

Sylvie laughs like I hoped she would.

"The point is to make your mom look like herself, but accentuated. Just like we did with you." I hold up the tube of pink. "So, Juna . . . ?"

10

PETER

KARA DOESN'T STOP WITH MY NIECE. SHE DOES MY SISTER'S makeup—light and barely there but enough to please both Sylvie and Juna—and then Mami's and even puts some lipstick on Grosi. And then Mami decides dinner is going to be formal this evening.

While I change into one of my suits, Kara helps my niece pick through her wardrobe and find something to wear.

I know that being a teenager is hard, and it's been exceedingly difficult on my sister's family as Sylvie transitions. I know from many late-night calls from Juna that hormone therapy, teasing from classmates, and dead naming are constantly nipping at the heels of the household's sanity.

So, for Kara to devote so much time and care into my niece felt like a miracle. I'm just an uncle; I don't truly understand the depths of what that family is going through, but when Sylvie cried, it broke me in some way.

Broke me enough to kiss Kara. It wasn't intentional, I don't think. It wasn't a sexy kiss; it was just driven by pure instinct and gratitude.

Afterward, though, when my thumb had stroked the soft

skin above her collarbone, and we'd stared at each other, I'd felt something stir.

I shake my head and slide my arms into my button-up.

There's a knock at the door. "Yes?"

"Um," Kara's voice wafts through the door. "It's me, can I come in?"

I look down. My shirt is half buttoned, and underneath, I've only got boxer-briefs on. "Just a moment." I grab the pants from the bed and pull them on while hopping across the room to the door. Kara's seen me in my underwear before, but this feels different, more intimate. We're about to sit down to dinner with my family, and I don't even know what the kiss earlier meant.

Zipping the pants up is loud, and Kara's right on the other side of the door, so I'm sure she heard. Nevertheless, I unlock and turn the knob, moving aside to let her in.

She glances down, and I look too. Only the top two buttons of my shirt are done, and it flares out from there, one side gaping open and exposing my belly and the trail of hair leading down to my waistband. It's gaping because the tail is down my pants and then out the zipper.

"Shit." I turn away and try to get the zipper down, but it's stuck. The white shirt hem is trapped in the teeth, I think, though I can't see it because I don't bend that way.

"Do you need help?" Kara asks, amused.

"No," I say and grunt, pressing harder on the zipper.

"Peter, stop." She grabs my elbow, jerking my hand away from the zipper. "Don't ruin it. I can help."

Kara kneels in front of me, and I nearly die. After waking up this morning, then the kiss, and now this . . .

My eye catches on the neckline of her top. That spot of skin that I smoothed earlier is right there. It would be so easy to place my hand there again and follow the arch of her neck up, to tangle my fingers in her hair.

Now my cock is getting hard, and Kara hasn't made any

progress, so I tilt my head back to glare up at the ceiling. This is what I get for not letting her spend the holidays alone? Her mouth is inches from my hardening dick, and the gentle brush of her fingers as she works at the zipper is not helping.

Finally, the metal clasp releases and the teeth slide down. I pull away before I can spring out of my fly and make my hard-on any more obvious.

Kara stands and retreats to the closet, giving me a moment to zip up my pants properly and finish buttoning my shirt. She's rifling through one of the garment bags and pulling out a maroon dress.

"I'm going to see if this fits your niece," she says, hanger in hand. I step aside to let her open the door, but she pauses, one hand on the knob, her face tilting up to look at me, a glint of teasing in her eyes. "You know, plenty of guys I work with get hard while we're working together. It's nothing to be embarrassed about. It's normal when someone's right there. However . . . " She pauses and leans in. "Not many of them have kissed me a few hours before."

With that, she smiles at me and exits the room.

I sigh and lean against the wall. This woman, this stupid crush, is not going away.

Eventually, sounds coming from downstairs pull me in: laughter, glasses clinking, dishes clattering. When I come into the back room, the fire is roaring and the table is dressed in a cloth and silver and fancy stuff I haven't seen in years, if ever.

At each setting are white plates rimmed with silver that I recognize as my parents' wedding china. The cutlery is the real silver; the pieces monogrammed with my grandparent's initials.

Sylvie comes up beside me. "Isn't it pretty?" she asks in Swiss-German, handing me two glasses of red wine. "Mami said this is yours and this is Kara's."

I take the glasses and look my niece over. The dress looks great on her, and Kara changed her makeup again to accommodate it. "You look stunning. Shit. Am I going to be meeting a boyfriend soon?"

Sylvie laughs. "*Noooo.* You know I won't look like this in real life," she says. "Plus"—she turns and lifts her arm to show me the side of her dress—"Kara had to take the sides in for it to fit me."

I talk out the side of my mouth. "Well, if you hadn't shown me, I wouldn't have known. You're not supposed to reveal secrets like that."

She spins, twirling the skirt with her enthusiasm.

I watch her, sipping my wine and leaning against the wall, out of the way, until there's movement by the hall. I turn my head to spot Kara coming in.

Her long, curly hair is up into a bun at the top of her head, soft and poofy. Her dress is black and fitted, ending mid-shin and with a square neck that exposes her olive skin. There are a few freckles on her shoulders that draw my eye as she walks toward me.

"This is for you," I say, before she can comment on my gaze, and offer her the glass of wine. When she takes it, I put my hand in my pants pocket. Kara leans a shoulder on the wall next to me, watching my family with a smile on her face.

Despite the emotional day Sylvie's had, she's bloomed. She's energetic and says more in one meal than I've heard her say in years. It's nothing profound; it's nothing to do with her transition or the way she feels in her body like this, but it's the small things that I've missed.

And the ripple effect through the family. Juna is glowing with pride, Grosi doesn't misgender Sylvie once, and my mother sits at the head of the table, reaching out to touch Kara in gratitude every chance she gets.

Back in our room after dinner, I turn the light off and rest my head on the pillow. Next to me, Kara lays on her side. When I turn my head, her eyes glint in the barely-there light.

"Thank you for today," I say. It would have been a normal,

quiet dinner. Mami served charcuterie with sourdough bread we'd baked earlier, challah, cuts of meat and cheese, spreads, olives, and anything else we found in the pantry. Of course, we finished with cookies, my family teasing me by picking out my worst cookies to eat and saving Kara's beautiful ones.

But it wasn't the meal itself that was amazing. Everyone was so happy, like magic, like a miracle had happened. My sister's family was relaxed and carefree in a way that made me notice how tense and difficult things had been before. The gravity of their life was in stark contrast.

"Don't thank me for being nice to your niece. That's a low bar."

"I'd like to think so, but it's not always the case." I don't want to tell Kara how badly I've failed my family in the past, so instead, I segue. "You're very good at your job."

She smiles. I can *feel* her smile, even though we aren't touching. "Thank you. I love what I do."

"I don't just mean with my niece," I continue. "I should have said this before, but hiring you made a difference in my life. You gave me confidence in the way I look. It's easy to know that something isn't right, that a piece of clothing doesn't look good or fit right or whatever it is, but it's an entirely different thing to know how to fix it and to see potential in other people."

Kara doesn't speak, so I turn my body toward her. "You do see the potential in people. And that's a real talent. It's not something that should be taken carelessly because—"

Her fingers touch me first, a light graze of the tips over my cheek, gliding along the stubble of my jaw until her thumb is right in front of my ear, the rest of her hand cupping the back of my head and applying gentle pressure as she moves toward me. Then her lips are on mine.

This is a press, a kiss in the truest sense of the word, but when she pulls back, Kara doesn't go far. I *hear* her lips parting, her inhale, sharp and strong, and feel her hesitation.

I close the space between us, letting my lips relax, and this time . . . this time it's different. Kara's lips are softer and open, and her nails dig into my scalp. There's a breathy moan, a wet noise, and I'm pressing up into her, taking her in my arms and rolling her gently onto her back.

This is so far beyond a kiss now. Kara's waist is hot in my grip, her chest pressing against mine in every rise and fall of desperate breathing. I want to align us further, slide between her legs and rock against her and . . .

Kara pulls back.

"Thank you for saying all that. It's . . . " She hesitates. "It's been harder than I thought it would be running my business. I knew you liked my work but hearing it out loud is different."

I'm not great with words. I know this. But I can show my appreciation in other ways.

So, I lean back in and kiss Kara again.

11

KARA

I WAKE UP WITH WARM, SOLID ARMS AROUND ME AND THE THICK blanket like a cocoon. Last night, Peter's whispered confession in the dark was a balm soothing over me. Why was it so hard for my family to get my job, but this man, who has barely worked with me, to be honest, could see it as bright as day? He could feel it.

Was my family just immune to it, having grown up with me interested in fashion and style? Like a frog in boiling water, were they immune to the change?

Peter stirs, pulling me even closer. He's hard behind me, his morning wood digging against my ass, and he puts his mouth to my neck to trail kisses up the side, nipping and dragging as he goes now that we're both awake.

I shiver, remembering last night's kisses. We'd made out until we were too tired to move and fell asleep cuddling.

I tilt my head, encouraging him. Peter hums, and his hands wander apart. His left hand emerges from under the pillow where it was curled up and skims from the ball of my shoulder to my breast, loose in his tee shirt. His right hand, which had been possessively braced around me, moves lower.

"Peter," I whisper.

"Merry Christmas Eve, Kara," he responds, breath warm on my neck.

His fingers play with the hem of the shirt, skimming my thighs, the soft hairs there making everything so sensitive. His mouth is open and wet on my neck, but when he backs off, cold air rushes in, making me shudder.

My nipples abrade on the shirt, and all I want is for Peter to pull it off me. I want skin on skin, his fingers inside me, his lips going lower.

Peter finally rucks my shirt up, passing it from one hand to the other to give him access to all of me. His palm brushes my belly, sweeps over my mound before pressing between my legs. His other hand palms my breast, letting his fingers slide over my tight nipples.

Peter's fingers press into me. He groans quietly when he feels how damp my panties are, and we roll together, both giving him more room to work. Peter bends his knee, and I match him, opening myself up to his fingers.

His dick is no longer pressed into the crack of my ass, but it's laying against one cheek. Putting my foot on the mattress, I can lift and roll my hips, not just against his fingers, but backward onto his cock.

Peter meets, thrusting up. His fingers find my clit through the cotton, and my breath gets ragged. Being sandwiched between his fingers and his thick length is driving me wild.

Him too. He's panting in my ear, his thrusting getting more and more erratic. I grip his forearms, both of them, and revel in the sharp breath he releases as my fingers dig into his flesh.

"Peter," I whisper, getting desperate and circling my hips harder. "Peter, Peter, oh god . . . "

There's a knock on the door, and we both tense. The doorknob rattles, and we spring into action, me tugging down the shirt and Peter pulling up the blankets that have slipped down.

"Yeah?" Peter calls.

The answer is in Swiss-German, and it's Noah's voice, excited and hopeful. "Onkel Peter? De Sturm ist verby. Mer wölle dusse spiele."

"He says the storm is over," Peter whispers to me. He raises his voice. "Noah, Kara and I need to get up and have breakfast first."

"But it's eight o'clock," he whines.

"We'll be down soon."

"Oh-kay." He draws it out, the resigned sigh of neglected niblings everywhere.

We listen to him slump down the stairs before meeting each other's eyes.

Peter smiles first, the corners of his eyes crinkling wonderfully in a way that makes my heart swoon. "We have time."

Morning breath be damned, I flop backward and pull Peter down on top of me. His mouth meets mine in a flurry of lips and teeth and tongue. This time, his hand shoots straight down inside my panties, a new sense of urgency driving us.

He plays my clit, rolling it between two fingers. When I can't kiss him anymore, too busy gasping and fighting to keep quiet, he migrates from my lips, kissing my chin, the spot right under my jaw, and then over to the side of my neck. "Can you come for me?" There's a note of pleading that undoes me.

"Just a bit harder. And more like . . . yeah."

I twist underneath him as the new pressure has me tensing. Peter's mouth on my neck is no longer just tasting and teasing, it's his body pinning me down, the points of his mouth and his fingers stretching me taut until I snap with a strangled cry.

Peter keeps moving his fingers, drawing it out for as long as he can while his mouth sucks and nips.

"Oh Jesus," I mutter when it gets to be too much, grabbing his hand and rolling toward him. I lay on my back, panting, while Peter eases his mouth and hand away from my sensitive skin and wraps his arms around me.

After a few minutes of him holding me, I run my hand across my forehead. Despite the cold of the room, we've both gotten sweaty.

But we're not done.

Peter's cock rests against my hip, still hard. When I look down, his underwear is pulled tight, straining against his erection, a darker spot in the fabric where he's leaking precome.

I reach across my body and grip him through his underwear. Peter groans, rolling away a bit to give me room to move.

His cock is solid and heavy, perfect in my hand. I give a few experimental strokes through his boxer-briefs and then delve inside. Peter shifts to help me, pushing the waistband down around his thighs.

When I get a firm grip and start to stroke, Peter tenses. His hands tangle in my hair, his lips press against my forehead. He mutters a few words I can't understand, his hips thrusting up to meet me. "Fuck, das isch so guet. Kara, meh, isch will meh . . . "

His body jerks, cum spilling out onto my stomach, a particularly strong burst hitting the underside of my breast, leaving a warmth that cools quickly. Peter's hands tighten on my head, and he grunts this beautiful, low sound just for me.

Just like he did, I keep stroking until he gets too sensitive and pulls away, twitching. He lands on his back, chest rising and falling.

This smile is the new favorite: carefree and satiated and secret.

It's the best one, and there won't be many more.

The thought is so sharp. If Noah is right, and the storm

has passed, it won't be long until the snow is cleared and the flights are back on.

But for now, it's Christmas Eve morning. I've got a gorgeous man next to me in bed who made me come.

Peter doesn't luxuriate next to me for long. He rises as soon as he's caught his breath and brings a shirt back and helps me wipe off my chest and stomach. He finishes with a wet, open-mouth kiss on my breast that makes me want to throw the covers back over us and start all over again.

But laughter sounds from downstairs, and Peter pulls back.

"Go shower if you want. I'll make you breakfast."

By the time I get downstairs, dressed in leggings and a slouchy sweater, the kitchen smells amazing already. Nora has made toast from the leftover bread, and Peter has a plate waiting for me at the table next to a steaming cup of coffee. His family all wishes me a merry Christmas Eve, and Juna surprises me with a bouquet of tissue paper flowers.

"We dug out some craft supplies last night to see what we could make you," she explains. "Sorry you have to spend the day with us instead of your family." She squints at me . . . or, not at me, exactly, but slightly lower and to the side. "You know, maybe I am not that sorry because you've got—" she drops her voice down to a whisper "—a bite mark on your neck."

"Jesus," I mutter and cover the left side of my neck with my hands.

"She does? Where?" Peter asks, leaning over the table to look.

"Well, I would guess exactly where you bit her, brother."

I undo my top knot and sweep my hair to one side. My cheeks heat, and I swat at Peter as he leans further to look. "You beast," I reprimand, but there's no heat behind it.

Juna saunters away. "I did not need to know this about my

brother. Oh, and if the kids see it, you have to explain," she calls over her shoulder as she leaves the room.

I hear Noah from the TV room. "See what?"

Peter and I look at each other. I melt when I see the warmth and affection in his eyes. My insides go all gooey and lovesick.

Nora joins us at the other end of the table. "Have either of you even noticed?" She gestures to the outside.

It's glorious out. Their backyard is covered in a beautiful, pristine blanket of snow, and the sky is clear blue and vibrant.

"I've already volunteered the family to help shovel sidewalks in the neighborhood. Tom and Liam are already out."

"We'll go," I tell her.

"Not you, it's Christmas Eve. Peter will go. You and I will bake cookies or read by the fire or whatever coziness you want."

I glance at Peter, who's watching me, trying not to smile while he eats his breakfast.

"Or maybe you'd like to be outside. Nice fresh air and all that."

Under the table, Peter hooks my ankle with his.

"Yeah," I say, glancing back at Nora. "Fresh air sounds good."

She throws a hand up and laughs. "Sure. Go enjoy 'fresh air.'"

Nora lends me her boots and a pair of snow pants. We step outside into the crisp, cold air.

The street is that same pristine white from the backyard, stretching out in either direction. The road curves up to the right and down to the left. Across from us, the ground rises, the rooftops of houses uphill barely visible over the bank of snow.

There are lumps there, too, huddling on the opposite side of the smooth, level road. Cars that no one is bothering to dig out, so they sit like molehills underneath the snow.

Liam has already begun shoveling the side of the road, and I can see the painted stripe that marks the sidewalk versus the street.

To the far right, in the distance, there's a hill. Most of it is covered in frosted, heavily laden trees, but there's a big chunk that is a mess of downed trees scattered like toothpicks.

"We're lucky we didn't lose power," I remark, lifting my chin to indicate the trees.

Peter bends over to pick up a shovel out of the snow. "Our power lines are mostly underground. It would take a lot to knock our power out."

"Oh," I say, and follow Peter, who's slung the shovel over his shoulder and walks opposite his dad, down a cleared path. It's slick, even in my borrowed boots, and twice I have to pinwheel my arms to prevent myself from busting my ass.

We catch up to Tom, wielding a shovel with an older man I don't know and speaking in Swiss-German and laughing. The house they stand in front of has an actual driveway, unlike Liam and Nora's house, so Tom is helping shovel out a wider area.

Peter shakes the man's hand and introduces me, but then they have a brief conversation in Swiss-German before Peter puts his hand on my back and guides us to keep walking downhill. When I nearly slip a few yards away, Peter moves his hand to grip my elbow.

"Mr. Meyer says, on account of it being almost Christmas, that we should not wish for a Christmas miracle but give one a little push."

At my questioning glance, he clarifies. "We're going to the town square. This is where the Christmas market is held, and usually, the last day is the 23rd, but because of the storm, it was closed. If everyone chips in to clear the snow and string the lights and assemble the stalls, we just might give you— and the rest of the town—one last night."

As if I'll have trouble remembering this Christmas. I lean

into Peter while the snow crunches under our boots. We have to stop occasionally to help neighbors who haven't quite finished their shoveling. The houses are fairly spaced out, and it's a lot of ground to uncover.

Then we reach a pedestrian bridge where lots of people are out with shovels and salt. The road is clear, and cars move on the opposite side of the river.

The town square is crowded. It's rectangular-ish, with one long side—I think facing the river, though I can't see it—where there are only the snow-covered tops of trees and roofs visible, and the other long side has several buildings rising up and streets running away from it and into the city. A large tent is being erected in the widest space, and volunteers assemble smaller booths between a neat row of bare trees.

Peter finds someone who looks responsible. She barks out some instructions, but Peter gestures at me. "She speaks English."

"Marina! Chum, und bring d'Frau an d'Büez!"

With a grin, Peter leaves me, trundling off with the shovel. A few moments later, a short, round woman about my age with a mass of curly hair that rivals mine and a delightful smattering of freckles across her cheeks approaches me. "Hello, I hear you're English. I'm Marina." She has an accent that might be British. I'm not sure.

"Hi, Marina. I'm Kara. American, actually."

"Good, come help me set up the lights."

I work for at least an hour, in which I climb up and down many a ladder, have snow fall from the trees directly into my mouth twice, and learn that Marina is from Wales and works for one of the restaurants nearby.

By the time Peter finds me, we've got the lights strung all the way around the square. Of course, it's daylight, so the lights aren't adding to the ambiance yet.

Most of the work now turns toward the individual booths

themselves, but I'm not much help with my non-existent Swiss-German. I follow Peter and help where I can.

Around noon, Marina shoos us away, and we trudge back across the river and up. The trip is much shorter now that the whole path is cleared, and we arrive at the house, strip our layers off, and sit down to soup hot off the stove.

12

PETER

AFTER LUNCH, PAPI AND I SPEND TIME IN THE BACKYARD. ONE of the younger trees was uprooted and has to be hauled out. We check the house's exterior for damage, and find none. While helping at the Christmas market, I'd always been able to hear Kara chattering away with Marina, even from across the square. There were so many times in my childhood that I found my sister or my mother annoying because they talked ad nauseum; with Kara, I find it endearing.

When I slip my outer gear off and climb the stairs, Kara is sitting on the bed cross-legged, head bowed over her phone, typing quickly.

I lean against the doorway, crossing my arms. "Hey."

She glances up and breaks into a smile. My stomach flips at the warmth in her eyes, and I step into the room, taking a seat on the bed. "I was thinking we'd light the menorah tonight with my family and then go to the Christmas market. Everyone wants to go, so it won't be just us, but we can eat there and enjoy it at our own pace."

"Yeah, that sounds great." She takes a deep breath, puffing her cheeks out before blowing a raspberry. "I just booked my flight home for tomorrow. The airport is open again. It's a

Christmas miracle." She says the last bit with false cheer, or maybe that's just what I'm hoping to hear.

Her eyes bounce back and forth between mine, reading me as I struggle to hold my disappointment. What did I think was going to happen? She can't stay here forever. She's got work and her family back in New York, and I've got mine here.

The storm has left, and so must she.

"I will take you to the airport, of course."

She dips her chin in a quick nod. "Thanks." She holds her phone up. "I was just telling my family about it. And catching up with Nash and Clara. Want to see their Christmas pajamas?"

"Their pajamas?"

Kara waves me to her, and I crawl up the bed and settle on the headboard next to her.

"Yeah, the family does a goofy Christmas pajamas tradition. The kids love it. They picked a theme this year: onesies."

She turns her phone around to show me a picture of Nash and Clara posing next to a tree while wearing green onesies with big, colored Christmas lights printed on them.

"Oh, and hang on." She swipes a few times through photos that look like a Hallmark Christmas movie until she lands on a photo of Clara's nephew, Ricky, wearing a reindeer onesie, complete with an antler hood.

"Apparently, Molly didn't realize that Ricky's had a hood, and she's *pissed* that her snowman doesn't. And obviously, that's a great reason for a six-year-old to throw a tantrum." She flips to the picture of Molly holding a carrot like a nose. Kara hums and leans her head against me. She gives a half-hearted flip through a few more photos.

There's a knock on the door, and Kara straightens up before answering. The door cracks open, and Sylvie peeks in. Her eyes dart between the two of us.

"Hey, Sylvie." Kara smiles. "What's up?"

Sylvie hesitates but then comes in holding something behind her back. "I wanted to ask you a makeup question."

"Oh, good." Kara gestures to my niece closer. "Lay it on me."

Sylvie brings her hands in front of her, and my heart drops into my stomach when I recognize the packaging. "These are old, but are they still good?"

Kara takes a few of the makeup cases from her. "Oh, this is a nice brand. And unopened? Yeah, these are totally still good. Once you open them, they should still last a while."

"Which ones would work best for me? Like how you did my makeup last night?"

Kara explains, tapping her nails on the cases as she talks, pointing out which of the makeups I bought for my niece would look good. She leans over, showing Sylvie exactly where and how to apply the makeup.

When they're done, Sylvie hugs Kara in thanks and jumps off the bed. Before she leaves the room, though, Kara calls to her. "Hey, where did you get that makeup? I thought you said you didn't have any."

Sylvie glances at me, and instead of sadness, she smiles. "Uncle Peter gave it to me."

When the door clicks shut, Kara backs up and sits against the headboard again. She nudges me with her elbow, a hint of a tease in her voice. "You gave her that stuff? It's a nice gift. I wonder why she didn't use it for a year."

When she sees my face, her smile falls. Kara reaches over to rub her hand on my arm. "What happened?"

I let my head thunk back.

"Last year, around this time, I'd been seeing a woman for a few months, and I brought her for one night with my family for the lighting of the menorah. We opened our gifts, and I'd gotten Sylvie that makeup set. She was so excited, and it was perfect until later that evening in the kitchen when my girlfriend said to me that she thought it was a waste of good makeup."

Kara gasps, and I glance at her. Her face goes from horror to indignation to sympathy. "Let me guess. Sylvie heard?"

I nod.

"Of course, she did," Kara mutters, shifting her gaze out over our toes. "That bitch."

The corner of my mouth flicks up in a smile. "I dumped her, obviously, but Sylvie was in such a tender spot, and it was so traumatizing. We encouraged her to try makeup, anyway, and to talk to her therapist about it. Hell, *I* talked to my therapist about it. I know that my girlfriend said those words, but I brought her. I was responsible for choosing to expose my family to her."

"Peter, it's not your fault." Kara leans in and threads her fingers through mine.

"I know." I squeeze my eyes tight against the heat building.

"But guilt isn't always logical," Kara says in understanding. She squeezes my hand. "Sylvie will be okay."

I swallow a thick pile of gratitude that she's here, that she's been so kind and wonderful to my family.

"What gave you the idea to give her makeup?"

"My mother gave us all books to read about raising transgender kids and transitioning. There was a lot to learn that I couldn't help with. But buying some nice makeup for her was something I could do. I went to a shop in Zurich, and one of the clerks helped me." He shakes his head. "I had brought some pictures, and they did their best."

"It was a great idea. Maybe next time, you could take her in with you and have her pick out stuff. And the staff will help her match her skin tones better if she's there in person. And I bet she'd love spending the time with you too."

I squeeze her hand and open my mouth to thank her, but I'm cut off.

"Uncle Peter," Noah shouts from below. "Grosi says you have ten minutes."

"Fuck," I mutter, letting go of Kara's hand and running both of mine over my face. "I better shower."

———

WE CAN SEE THE GLOW AND HEAR THE MARKET BEFORE WE TURN the last corner. Kara's hand is in mine, keeping us together while we move with the crowd that separates us from the rest of my family. Noah was bouncing off the walls, excited to "celebrate Christmas," and my dad grumbled the entire walk over about Christmas taking over December. It's not as busy as it usually is since there aren't many tourists, but there are still plenty of people excited to be outside after the storm.

"Oh my god," Kara says when the market comes into view. "It's so quaint."

Big, warm lights string from tree to tree and over rooftops. There are piles of snow banking the square, but the interior is cleared and well-trodden. The air smells of thick spices and sugar. I stop to buy us two mugs of glühwein, the hot mulled wine that Kara says smells like Christmas in a cup.

She shops while we walk, which means I end up carrying several bags of stuff before she realizes I need a hand to eat. We solve that problem by parking her on one of the hay bales while I retrieve food. I bring her back a variety—from apple fried doughnuts to potato pancakes and a small paper plate that overflows with toast and raclette—hot cheese scraped off of a wheel and topped with onions and spices.

"This is like a heart attack waiting to happen," she says, a strand of melted cheese caught on her bottom lip. She licks it off.

"I'm not too worried about it," I say. "We'll work it off later."

Kara laughs loudly, causing a couple near us to turn and

look. Her cheeks are flushed, her hair escaping the bun on her head in tendrils. She eyes me and hums appreciatively. "You're goddamn right we will."

I lean over and kiss her. She tastes like cheese and salt and heat.

When I pull back, Kara's eyes glint. "I like this smug and confident Peter."

"Good. He likes you too."

Kara takes another bite of the raclette. Her eyes dance over the crowd, the lights, the trees, the couples and families bundled up and having fun together. When she swallows, she brings up the question we've both been avoiding. "He likes me, even though I'm flying home tomorrow?"

Her job, her family, her life are back in New York. We've been in a snow-filled, isolated world. She's leaving. I'm staying.

"Even though you fly home tomorrow."

Kara hums and finishes her raclette. She dusts her hands off and rises to her feet. "Tomorrow's coming pretty fast. We better put the time we have left to good use." She offers me her hand, and I take it.

13

KARA

WE FIND PETER'S FAMILY AT AN OUTDOOR TABLE. EVERYONE IS bundled up and drinking a hot beverage, even Peter's grandmother.

"You've shopped up a storm," Juna comments, eyeing the bags we're carrying.

"Yes, I have, and we're going to head back to the house before I buy more and break my pack mule." I pat Peter's shoulder.

"Mama, darf i au göhe?" Noah asks. Peter and his sister share a look.

"No, you can't go. We're having family time."

"But Peter and Kara are going back. And we do this every year." His tone gets whiny.

Juna glances at us, and there's a spark of laughter in her eyes. She holds in her hands the potential to cock-block us with her ten-year-old kid. "If you go back with Peter and Kara, you can't do stuff with them. Kara has to pack for tomorrow. You'll have more fun here. You haven't even had a Grittibänz yet."

"Mamaaaaaaaa."

"Noah, stop. Du bisch zu alt, um disch so zu benehme."

Peter glances at me, raising an eyebrow and throwing me a look that says *Kids? Whatcha gonna do?*

"It's fine," I say quickly.

"No." Juna is firm. "He stays with us. But thank you. Noah, you have to hang out here for thirty more minutes. Thirty. Minutes," Juna reiterates while her gaze flicks between Peter and me. "Now try to fit as much fun as you can into that time, and then we'll all go home." Juna smirks at her own cleverness.

We say goodbyes, and Peter guides me out of the Christmas market, and as the noise and smells fade, he picks up the pace.

"Have I told you I love your sister?"

He chuckles. "I could guess based on the two of you reading together. She is pretty great."

We cross the bridge over the river, and Peter braids his fingers through mine. We both have gloves on, but Peter's hand is big and warm, even through the knitting.

"Should we set a timer?" I joke. "A sex timer?"

"It's been a while since I had to work with a sex deadline."

"A deadline! Ha. Where has this wry sense of humor been hiding? Does Nash know you're funny?"

He shrugs, looking away, but I can tell the compliment pleases him.

"I'll tell him you should emcee the next Heartly event," I tease.

"Fuck no," Peter groans.

I clear my throat and drop my voice to try to mimic Peter's. "Ones and zeros. Boolean. HTML."

Peter throws his head back, laughing. Oh god, his Adam's apple just peeks over the scarf he's wearing. I would try to make him laugh for the rest of my life just to watch that.

"Do you even know what you are saying?" He nudges me.

"I'm speaking your language." I nudge him back a little

harder. We're coming up to a house with a small snow-covered lawn. "Don't I sound so smart?" I ask, and then I hip-check him onto the snow.

But I miscalculate and don't get his hand out of my grip fast enough. He squeezes and pulls me down with him onto the lawn.

No, not just with him. On top of him.

I bounce slightly with his laughter, and my weight has tugged the scarf down, exposing that Adam's apple right at my eye level.

I kiss it, and Peter groans. It moves under my mouth as he swallows, and then he's pulling me toward him, taking my mouth in his. I thread my hands into his hair and the snow, pressing *deeper, hotter, more.*

A light turns on inside the house that belongs to this lawn, and we both look up. There's someone moving around inside, so I roll off Peter, and we both rise to our feet. He grabs my hand, and we walk faster.

By the time we get to the house, I'm sweating in my layers, warmed from the inside out with the mulled wine, exercise, and attention from Peter. We both strip down, jackets hung up, boots in a neat row, gloves and hats and scarfs in a basket. I'm wearing jeans and a loose cotton shirt, and goosebumps break across my skin as the cool air inside the house washes over me.

That is, until Peter presses into me, backing me up against the door and putting his mouth on mine in a hard kiss. His hands grip my hips, finding the hem of my shirt and rucking it up. They slide up my sides, over my ribs to the edge of my bra, and then back down.

Mine are in his hair, pulling him, holding him to me. Peter's nose is delightfully chilly as it nudges mine, his hair slightly damp from our roll in the snow.

His hands move down and grab my ass, lifting me. I wrap my legs around his waist, my arms around his neck, and hold on as he moves through the house and down the stairs.

"It's probably way safer for you to put me down."

He grunts.

"If we spend our allotted sex time in the emergency room, I'm going to be pissed."

"Shut up. I like holding you."

Thank god the stairs are carpeted. I figure we are out of the danger zone now that we're on the right floor and kiss Peter again. He's clumsy as he tries to kiss me and walk us to his bedroom, but we get there and the room tilts and I let go. I'm on my back on the bed, and Peter's kissing his way down my body. My shirt comes off, and he kisses along the edge of my bra.

I run my hands over his shoulders, shoulders I've touched professionally but haven't been able to caress like I yearn to. I grab at the back of his shirt, a polo in a winter green color that I adore, tugging to get it out of his pants and over his head.

He gets stuck—I forgot about the buttons in the front. "What the—"

"Hang on, let me get it back down."

We wrestle for a few moments before I get the hem down.

"Do you not know how clothes work?" His eyes are wide, mock-surprise. He even gives me a teasing head tilt.

"No, but I've got this terrible client who does his buttons up like a dork." I get the top one undone.

"Maybe I am a dork. Or I'm just too cool for Americans." He kisses me once, hard, distracting me. "What's the point of buttons if you aren't supposed to do them up?"

I don't bother answering, just undo the last button and attempt to get his shirt over his head again. This time it works, and I run my hands over the smooth expanse of his back, over those broad shoulders.

We spend some time exploring exposed skin with our hands and mouths. I love the way my palms glide down his back, the way my fingers can dig into that channel at his spine, feeling the muscles flex and move on either side. His waist is narrow, his chest covered in dark, soft chest hair. When I smooth my palm over his nipple, he jerks and then retaliates by pulling my bra cup down and wrapping his lips over my nipple.

The heat of his mouth sends a flush over my whole chest. He settles between my legs, all his focus on me. I thread my fingers through his hair, shifting against him.

He takes time that we probably don't have, but it feels so good. Each swipe of his tongue, the slight suction, the fanning of his breath over my skin.

The cool air replaces his mouth as he pulls back to take my bra completely off and focuses on my other breast.

After a few glorious minutes, I get antsy for more. I tug his hair lightly and raise my head. "Peter."

He looks up, mouth swollen and eyes dark.

"I'm not exactly fast, and I don't know how much time we have left, so . . . "

"Got it." He rears up between my legs, unbuttoning my jeans, and with quick, efficient moves, pulls them off me. He bends over, pressing a kiss directly above my clit over my underwear, a black cotton thong. It makes me jerk slightly, and he backs away, pulling the scrap of material down and off.

He lies belly-down on the bed, still in his jeans. He smooths his hands over the insides of my thigh, pulling my legs further apart.

"What do you like, Kara?" The words are low against my skin, pressed into my soft inner thigh.

I swallow. My voice comes out rough anyway. I *love* that he asked. "Lots of tongue. Can you spread me and put a finger or two in?"

Peter wraps an arm around my leg, his palm landing on my mons. His thumb and forefinger pull my lips back and expose my clit to his gaze. Then his eyes flit up to mine, and he puts the middle two fingers on his other hand in his mouth, lubricating them.

My head falls back. *Jesus.* Who knew this man had so much filth inside of him? Who knew eye contact was that fucking sexy?

I'll think about all the terrible life decisions that led me to be surprised by that later. For now, I focus on the warm breath and the probing finger that carefully slips inside of me. I rock my hips, wanting it deeper.

Peter groans. "Dis is so gopferdammi heiß."

He's watching. I involuntarily squeeze him, and am rewarded with another finger.

"Keep your fingers still," I pant. "Please."

He does. Then his mouth covers me, and his tongue goes to work. My fingers run through his hair as he experiments for a while until he does something just right, and I gasp. "That, right there."

I glance down. His eyes are closed, his hips raised, his face relaxed. I let my head fall back again and focus on the building orgasm.

Within a few minutes, my legs and abs tighten, my body curls up, and I'm coming on his face. I cry out his name and ride it for as long as I can.

When I finally go slack, Peter gently pulls his fingers out and slows his tongue, switching to tender kisses.

I nudge him with my knee. "Do you have any condoms?"

He pulls away and smiles up at me, his mouth and chin glistening. "Yes." He climbs off the bed, grabbing his shirt and wiping his face before stripping off his jeans. I roll onto my side and prop my head up with a hand to watch while he digs out a condom and a small bottle of lube from his suitcase. He rolls the condom on and slicks himself up.

"I hope I didn't take too long," I say as he rolls me over and crawls up my body.

"Worth it." He guides his cock to press into me. We both watch as he slides in to the hilt.

I wrap my legs around his waist and run my hands up his arms. He shifts, the muscles in his abs popping out when he rolls his hips.

He drops to his elbows, caging me in, and we share a deep, long kiss.

Which is why we hear the front door open and a loud voice call out, "Peter! Kara! We're home!"

"Fuck," Peter curses.

He withdraws and points at me. "Stay here."

I roll over to my side again and watch as Peter cleans up quickly and pulls his pants on, hopping toward the door.

I make sure I've covered before he exits, and then I flop back onto the bed. A few minutes later, the door opens, and Peter enters again. "I told them you were packing. Everyone's downstairs, playing a game." He sits on the edge of the bed and strips off the pants again. "They let Noah pick the game."

I lift the covers, quirking an eyebrow and showing Peter I'm still naked. "We can be quiet."

He crawls toward me and then freezes. He sags, putting his head in both hands. "That was my only condom."

His hands fall, and we both look at the trash bin.

Ew.

Damn it.

I sit up, bunching the duvet at my waist. "I was tested a few months ago. I haven't slept with anyone since. And I've got one of those birth control implants." I point at my underarm.

"I haven't slept with anyone since I broke up with my ex last December. I got tested at my annual physical in March." He moves his hand to mine and squeezes. "Are you sure?"

"Yeah. I've never had sex without a condom. But I want to."

Peter stretches up to kiss me. It's soft and sweet, intimate in a new way. He tugs the duvet down and slips into the bed. His fingers glide down my body as I lie back. They slip through me, the lube still working its magic.

He positions himself and presses in. Without the condom, it's more slick heat and soft skin, but most of all, it's the way we look at each other. Trusting.

I return my legs to around his waist, and he drops to his elbows, smoothing my hair back from my face. He rocks, and I let out the tiniest whimper.

"Shh." He kisses me, still moving inside me. "You feel so good, Kara."

Our breath mingles, he shifts and pulls, and I can't help the noises that escape me.

Peter shushes me again. His mouth moves to my ear. "I thought you said you could be quiet."

"I'm trying," I whisper, and then bite my lip.

I'm good at being quiet during solo time—hello, I live with my parents—but having Peter's bare cock inside me and his warm body over mine is so much better.

When I make another noise, Peter stops, choking back his laughter. His voice drops. "Am I going to have to gag you?"

It's a tease, the humor in his voice, but it still makes me clench around him.

He pulls back, looking me in the eye, serious now. "Would you like that?"

"I . . . I guess I never thought about it. I am wondering, though, what exactly you plan to gag me with." I pat his sides as if looking for pockets, and he laughs.

This right here is intimacy in a way I've never experienced before—his cock inside me, us both bouncing slightly while we struggle to control our laughter, his barely-contained smile pressing into mine because how can we *not* kiss right now?

But then the laughter fades, and we're left staring into

each other's eyes. Peter moves a hand from my hair to palm my mouth, his thumb stroking my chin.

"Tap if you want me to stop," he says.

My eyes roll back a little because having his weight press into me, my nostrils flaring out and my teeth pressing into my lips, is a whole other level of hot.

I'm not sure it's muffling much but I like it. Peter thrusts, slow and steady, and I dig my heels into his ass to encourage him, but he won't rush. He's in control, and I'm not.

His brow wrinkles in concentration, his lips part in pleasure. The duvet slips down, and then he kicks it off as we overheat.

Peter's palm shifts. The pressure against my mouth eases and his gaze drops down to my mouth. One finger twitches, and then his middle finger pulls back far enough to nudge at my lips. I open.

I don't know if I throb or his cock twitches or both. His middle finger curls inside my mouth and I suck as Peter's head drops down to the pillow beside me.

He closes his lips around my earlobe as he stiffens and comes, barely making any noise at all.

I wish, briefly, that I'd had foresight. That when my flight had gotten canceled, I had turned to him and said, "Let's get a hotel room. Let's spend this storm tearing each other apart and building ourselves back together, loud and wild and reckless."

But we won't get to do that. Because tomorrow, I'm flying home.

14

PETER

Kara's alarm goes off early. Last night, we had laid in bed, reminiscing over the last few days as if they were nostalgic, sepia-toned memories dug out of the attic of our minds. Then I'd made her come again using my hands, and fucked her from behind with a slow, measured pace that made us both tremble. She'd been quieter that time, maybe because it was late and our bodies were tired.

I'd forgotten how good sex without a condom was, but everything else was heightened too. The press of my hand against her mouth, the ridge of her teeth against her lips, the way her chin pushed against my thumb when she came on a silent scream.

And now I have to drive her to the airport.

We go downstairs. Papi is already awake, drinking coffee in the back room, the backyard still dark. We make bowls of yogurt and muesli, sipping our coffee, needing that artificial jolt because we didn't get enough sleep last night.

Mami comes in and slides a cellophane bag of cookies— Kara's best ones—across the counter. She hugs Kara from behind, and Kara smiles.

"Thank you for having me."

"Of course. Travel safe, and take care of my boy."

I look away, gathering our bowls and taking them to the kitchen. Kara goes upstairs to finish packing, and Mami goes back to bed.

"The streets have been cleared," Papi says. "I heard the snowplows last night."

"Good."

Papi's always been the best person to be around when I'm not in the mood to talk. He goes back to his book while I wash the dishes.

By the time I'm done, Kara's ready. Papi helps me load the luggage and gives Kara a quick hug.

The sky is a softer black by the time we make it onto the A1. Kara stares out the window, her profile barely visible in the beams of oncoming cars and street lights.

On the drive to my parents' house, prior to the storm, I'd been so nervous that I'd be ruining our holidays again, that any progress my sister's family had made would be destroyed by hurtful words—or careless ones.

Instead, what I got was an insight into this bright, accepting woman who gives people confidence to be themselves and tenderness when they don't believe they can. The care she gave my niece, the bonding with my sister, the help she gave my mother.

This can't be it.

Three days with Kara, and I ache at the prospect of saying goodbye.

We've been avoiding talking about it, but time is running out. My stomach flips as I slow the car and pull over to the shoulder. Cars whizz past, but we're still in the outskirts of the city, a bank of snow-covered bushes blocking the view of patchwork farmland.

Kara stares at me.

"When can I see you again?"

"I . . . " Kara's mouth opens. "I don't know. Do you have any plans to come to the US?"

"No." I don't travel much for work anymore since most of the team works remotely. And the trips I do take are usually to our offices in London or Salisbury. "What about you? Do you have many clients here?"

Kara shakes her head. "I got you because of Nash. Most of my clients are in New York."

"If I came to New York, could I see you? I can come, maybe once a month? I don't want this to be over."

Kara thinks, her eyes staring past the windshield at some distant point.

"I could fly you over here, too."

After an excruciatingly long pause, Kara turns back to me. "Have you ever been in a long-distance relationship?"

"No. Have you?"

"Not since college. It didn't go well, but we were young and dumb. But flying back and forth every month is a huge commitment. And my work schedule is wild. I hardly even make it home for dinner with my parents half the time I say I will. You'd fly all the way over, spend money on a hotel room because I live with my parents, and then you might not even see me because a client gained five pounds over their vacation and their dress won't fit anymore or their pregnant wife throws up in the car on the way to a gala and they need a backup outfit. Both of which have happened before, by the way."

"There are other options."

"Like what?" Kara's eyebrows draw together. "We live thousands of miles apart. Our *jobs* are thousands of miles apart and very different."

Her job is in New York, but does it have to be? "What if you could get clients here? I could introduce you to people. Nash knows all these rich, corporate types. We could help you rebuild your business. There's the global fashion industry right across the Alps in Italy."

Kara's face has fallen even further. "I could just . . . *rebuild my business?*" There's a sharpness in her tone I don't expect. "It would be easy for me because *you and Nash* would *introduce me to people?* Peter, my job is more than who I know. It's more than just a friend asking a friend to let me play dress up with them."

Kara folds her arms on her chest, her expression flat. "I've put so much into my business. New York fashion is cutthroat, and you're asking me to start from the ground all over again? I'm not asking you to give up your family, so don't ask *me* to throw away everything I've worked so hard for."

Her anger hangs in the air, and I tighten my grip on the steering wheel, turning away from her and staring out the front of the car.

I want to open my mouth and say that that's not what I meant. But I don't know what I *did* mean. She's right. I have no idea what it would take for her to move her business, for her to start over.

Especially when I can't offer that myself. The thought of leaving Switzerland, of not seeing my parents and their too-small home every week, or not spending time with my niece and nephew, helping my sister when Tom works long shifts at the hospital, or watching Sylvie build confidence and self-love . . . leaving my family isn't something I can do. Not for feelings that have moved so fast they scare me.

I look at the steering wheel and swallow my hopes of seeing Kara again. "Sorry," I say and shift back into Drive.

We don't talk on the rest of the drive. When I pull up to the terminal, Kara jumps out. I hustle to meet her at the trunk and grab bags while she retrieves a cart.

When everything's waiting at the curb, I touch her elbow.

"Kara, I am truly sorry." And I am. I have never been so careless with my words as I have this morning.

Her shoulders slump, and she exhales. "I know. Thank you for apologizing."

A car honks somewhere down the line, and I take one last risk. I step closer and put my hands on either side of her head, smoothing back the curls that have escaped her bun. I press a kiss to her forehead. "You are wonderful," I whisper in Swiss-German.

And then I step away.

———

BACK AT MY PARENTS' HOUSE, I GO RIGHT TO MY ROOM AND collapse onto the bed. Based on the noises coming from the kitchen, Juna and her family are up and eating. I got so little sleep last night, and I am so emotionally drained that I shut my eyes and immediately fall asleep.

When I wake up, it's bright outside and the house is quieter. Downstairs, my sister is in the back room, reading on the couch, a steaming mug on the table beside her.

"Where is everyone?" I ask, my voice dry and croaky.

Juna glances up and smiles at me. "Morning, sunshine. Tom is at work, Papi took Grosi back to her place, and then our parents took the kids to the park. There's an inter-sibling snowman competition."

I grunt and turn around, heading into the kitchen. Annoyingly, Juna follows.

"Ah, back to grunting now. Kara's gone, I assume?"

Because my head is in the fridge and Juna can't see me nod, I say, "Yes."

"I like her a lot." She shifts to give me room to pull out a platter of leftovers and goes around to the other side of the counter and takes a seat, grinning because, no doubt, I'm being extra grumpy today and that always amuses her. She hands me the loaf of leftover bread when I gesture for it. "She was great with the kids, fun, has great taste in books. She's very kind."

"As Kara told me this weekend, often, our family has a low bar for kindness."

Juna sobers. "I don't know about that. I like to believe in the good in people, but sometimes the world is not a kind or easy place."

I don't disagree, so I say nothing.

"Well, I enjoyed getting to know her, and I'm glad you brought her home. Plus, those gifts she gave us were so sweet."

I pause while smearing mustard on a slice of bread. "What gifts?"

Juna leans forward. "We all got emails this morning giving us books. Mami got a cookbook, Papi got a spy novel, I got some romances that Kara was horrified to learn I hadn't read, Noah got a book about science experiments, and Sylvie got a few YA romance novels, including one with a trans lead which—" she smacks her forehead "—why didn't I think of that?"

Fuck, Kara is so caring and kind and, if possible, I just fell even more in love with her.

Love.

My knife clatters on the counter when I drop it. Three days holed up with my family in a snowstorm, and I've fucking fallen in love.

"Oh lord. That's a serious epiphany going on there."

I squeeze my eyes shut and shake my head. "I wanted to see Kara again. I told her I'd fly to see her or that she could move here, and I'd help her rebuild her business. But her family lives in New York, and asking her to move was stupid."

"Um, why can't you move there? You mostly work remote, and Heartly has an office in New York."

I stare at my sister. "Because I don't want to leave my

family behind. You live here. You are the most important part of my life."

"We are, for now." She leans forward, clasping my hand in hers. "You know I love you and our parents. But if Tom was offered a job he wanted, if we had to move to make him happy, I would do it in a heartbeat. Most families don't grow up as close as we do. And while I love having you around to take care of our parents or spend time with my kids, I don't want you to sacrifice your own happiness and the opportunity for you to have love—the kind of love that brings out deeply buried joy inside of you, the kind of love that has you laughing and smiling and mooning over someone—just because you want to be near us."

Could I move to New York? Could I stand to see my family once or twice a year? Is it worth taking the risk, hoping that Kara's willing to be with me?

In our discussion this morning, I never thought to ask if I could move to be with her. But she also never said she didn't want to be with me—just that she didn't see how it could work.

She may not love me yet. But I'm not ready to let go.

I spin around, racing out of the kitchen and up the stairs to my room, where my phone waits. Nash answers on the third ring.

"If I were to move to New York, would there be a job for me?"

15

KARA

"Du bisch wundervoll" echoes over and over again in my head while I wait in line, check my bags, and get to my gate. I honestly thought it would be the feel of Peter inside me, the way his hand covered my mouth, the bounce of his laugh over me, that would get stuck in my mind. Instead, it's three simple words.

I don't speak Swiss-German, but I know enough to know "du" means you and "wundervoll" means wonderful, and I can piece together the rest.

You are wonderful.

I get plenty of compliments. My sisters, leaving their kids behind while I babysit, tell me I'm a godsend. My clients tell me I do a great job. Even *I love you*, ultimately the best compliment ever, is thrown generously around my family because, of course, we do love each other.

But after spending time with Peter's family, the rawness of all the feelings and the awareness of being *seen*, this simple compliment shoots into my chest and strikes a fire deep inside me that maybe I'd forgotten existed.

From the gate, I text my family that I'm on my way. I board the plane and fall asleep shortly after takeoff.

When I wake up, I connect my phone to the in-flight internet, and it vibrates with a message in my group chat with Bea and Clara.

CLARA

I emerged from the Christmas Chalet Utopia Fog—but only briefly to wish you all a Merry Christmas. I hear the airports are open again. Kara, are you flying home? Bea, did you survive the cabin?

BEA

I did. We're driving back after breakfast. The cabin is finally wearing our parents down. They have been less resistant to the idea of going somewhere else next year.

And by less resistant, I mean they protest at about 95% volume versus their usual 100%.

It has a lot to do with how ratty this rental cabin is getting.

And about one-third of the unrepaired damage over the years is due to us.

Which—we paid for damages, obviously.

KARA

I'm on the plane.

CLARA

How was time with Peter's family?

Magical, I type before I delete it. Life-altering, rule-breaking, paradigm-shifting.

KARA

I slept with Peter.

CLARA

Aksddrkjdfvu

!!!!!

Bea sends the gif of Andy Dwyer from Parks and Recreation staring at the camera in giddy shock. Clara sends a gif of Steven Colbert in front of a big sign that says, "I told you so!"

KARA

You did not.

CLARA

Excuse me, I was talking to Bea.

BEA

You did tell me so. All bow before the master.

But honestly, even a blind squirrel finds a nut every once in a while. You think everyone is into everyone.

CLARA

I do not!

BEA

It's because you're paired up, and you want everyone to be in a couple.

And you also want to double date with someone other than your dads.

Honey, you wanted me to ask out the courier who's like twenty years old, bless his heart. Where would we go? He can't drink!

CLARA

He's cute. And I swear to god, he's into you.

BEA

ANYWAY.

Back to Peter. Was it good? Are you going to do it again?

CLARA

Is he coming to New York?

KARA

Yes. No. And no.

He offered to, but then also said I should
move to Zurich.

CLARA

Oh, is that what you're going to do? There's
so much banking over there. I'm sure there's
some Swiss version of finance bros who
need someone to tell them how to dress.

KARA

Of course not. I can't give up my entire
business and move to Zurich. We first kissed
like three days ago. Do you know how
bonkers that sounds?

BEA

Wait, why would you be giving up your
business?

KARA

Because most of my clients are in New York.

BEA

Right, but it's not like all or nothing. And it's
not like you would have to move
RIGHT NOW.

And sure, you just kissed three days ago
and, one assumes, had lots of vigorous and
satisfying sex since then . . . ?

CLARA

It's like there's long term v short term, right?

Don't focus on the long term. Look at the
short term. Do you want to see Peter again?
If he flew to the city to take you out next
weekend, would you go?

KARA

Of course, I would.

BEA

Wow, was that a trans-Atlantic eye roll?

CLARA

I felt it.

Look, it's something to think about.

You kick ass in New York. You would kick ass everywhere.

The whole lesson that got me as happy and successful as I am with Nash and Worth Going is that sometimes you have to be flexible and pivot to get what you really want.

What I really want. Sex has muddled my brain. Fantastic sex and *you are wonderful.*

For the rest of the flight, I watch TV and get a flurry of messages in my family chat. They are bickering over the logistics of getting everyone back together for a second Christmas, with my mom asking everyone to pick up food on their way in. I have emails from Juna thanking me from the whole family for the gifts I sent them this morning.

At JFK, I wrestle my bags into a cab and text my family, giving them my ETA. Since it's Friday and everyone is off work today, we're meeting at my parents' house to play games and open the last of the presents.

The city is gray and chilly, but the streets are barren of snow, and instead of contending with pristine white snow-banks, I'm stuck in traffic on the expressway and gazing out at the cold, dark East River.

New York is lovely for Christmas in some places. And I bet Baden isn't as charming and idyllic all winter long as it was with a fresh coat of snow.

The cab pulls up in front of the single-family home my

parents have lived in for twenty years. There's a wrought-iron fence around the small yard and driveway, a few kid's toys in the brown grass, and Christmas lights around the border of every window and door. Mom is staunchly a colored light Christmas decorator, which we disagree on.

As the trunk of the cab pops, the front door opens.

"There she is!" Dad cries out. The whole family comes out, and I hug everyone as they grab luggage and pull me inside.

"Have you eaten yet?" Mom asks once I'm deposited at the kitchen counter. My parents renovated it a few years ago, and the kitchen is modern, white, stainless steel, and marble.

I shake my head. Mom pulls out leftovers and makes me a plate while my sisters and brothers-in-law ask me about the trip. I'm handed a toddler—India, Daria's three-year-old—for some inexplicable reason since I have to eat soon.

I worried that retelling the story—excluding the spicy bits, of course—would make it sound less magical, but it doesn't. The cozy evenings, the way the Toch family welcomed me in, the Christmas Market—they still sound as wonderful as they were.

"What an adventure you had," Daria says, taking her daughter back when Mom sets a hot plate down on the counter in front of me. The rest of the kids have been put down for naps or are parked in front of the TV with Stan, Nev's husband.

"All this because you had an in at Heartly." Tanya shimmies her shoulders and does a victory dance.

It's an innocuous comment, the kind she makes all the time. But after the week I've had, it's like a pea under my bed that I've finally realized I don't *have* to live with anymore. I think of Peter's family and how loving and supportive of each other they are, and all I'm trying to do is have a job that I love and occasionally make a difference in people's lives, and my family can't even give me that. I put my fork down before I've even had a chance to take a bite of Mom's casserole.

"No, it's not because I have an in at Heartly. It's because I'm good at my job."

My tone is sharp enough that she stills and her eyes go wide. "Well, yeah, but—"

"No buts. Every time we talk about my successes, you always bring up the fact that I got a big break because of you."

Her eyes flash. "It's not every time."

"Well, it feels like it to me, and that's enough."

"Kara," Mom chides. "She doesn't mean anything by it."

"Then why say it? You all do this. Nev is always telling me that family is the most important thing when she's asking me to babysit, and yeah, it is important, but taking care of my niece when you have other options isn't as important as my job. And Mom and Dad, you've constantly told me that I should have chosen a different career path. I'm doing what I love, and I wish you—all of you—would support that."

"We paid for your college and let you live under our roof," Dad argues.

"Yeah, you did. I succeeded because of the things you did. But I also succeeded *in spite* of the things that you did."

In the shell-shocked quiet of the kitchen, I stand up and push away from the counter. "I'm going to go for a walk."

One of my nieces laughs at the TV, and I grab my coat from the hook by the door, throwing it on. Then I have to put on gloves and a hat and, geez, storming out in the winter doesn't quite have the same effect as it does in the summer.

I even forget my phone.

I walk to the park, which doesn't make me feel any better because it's brown and ugly right now. I sit on a bench anyway and consider my options. I'm twenty-eight years old and still living with my parents, but rent in the city is hella expensive. I have a job that I excel at *despite* my family, but I can't do it this way anymore.

I need to move out. I need to set better boundaries with my family.

And maybe Clara is right. Maybe I can find a way to keep doing what I love while holding on to someone who believes I'm wonderful.

———

When Clara and Nash arrive back in New York from their chalet, Clara and I commandeer an empty meeting room in Heartly's office.

"This is very professional," Clara says when I pull out my laptop and set it on the table.

"I did ask if you could give me business advice."

"I know. And I'm flattered." She splays her hands out in front of her, palms up. "Welcome to Clara's Consulting and Coaching. How may I assist you?"

"I was hoping you could help me figure out how to pivot my business."

Clara claps her hands together. "Would this have anything to do with our favorite Heartly introvert?"

My cheeks heat. "Maybe."

"Ugh. I'm so happy for you." Clara squeezes me in a hug and then gets down to business by making grabby hands. "Okay, gimmie numbers, gimmie spreadsheets. Let's figure this out."

We spend hours going over the data, mostly because it takes that long to pull the information together and present it to Clara's satisfaction. What we finally get is a far cry from the hodge-podge of invoices and receipts that I usually panic bundle on April 1st and send to my accountant for tax purposes.

It takes so much time that Bea comes in after Nash has gone home and brings us cans of sparkling wine. All three of us look at how much business I bring in virtually and how much I do in person. Clara gives me some advice about driving more traffic to my website, some tips which have been helpful to her running *Worth Going,* and Bea suggests I reach out to my existing client base and ask them for virtual referrals. I've always asked my clients to pass my contact information along, but mostly, it was to people they knew through work or charity events locally.

Virtual clients are a bigger percentage of my revenue than I thought—look at me, using words like revenue—but they're still less than half my business. But having the numbers gives me a good idea of where I'll be if I drop all my in-person events.

Which I don't *have* to do, as Bea pointed out.

I walk out of Heartly's office more confident that I can figure something out and, also, glad to count some business-savvy, organized women as my best friends.

My euphoria builds even more when I see a text from my sister. I open it while heading toward the subway.

DARIA

Okay, please don't hate me, but could you watch the kids at Mom and Dad's on the 3rd? I swear I have a good reason: we're interviewing nannies. Not someone full-time, but someone who can come in and help in the mornings, especially to make it easier to get out of the house every day.

We decided that would be the best way to get some help and stop our entire days from being so stressful.

And I know that you probably have important work things to do, and I wouldn't ask, but Mom has her book club, and Dad is going to Poughkeepsie that weekend.

So I'm a little desperate. Again.

I check my calendar and message her back.

KARA

I can move an appointment.

I'm glad you've found a long-term solution.

DARIA

Thanks. You are the best.

I twist my lips to the side. Hearing my sister say I'm the best is nice. Not as great as hearing from Peter that I'm wonderful, but I'll take it.

I put a smutty audiobook on and navigate my way home. When I walk through the front door, I nearly run into Nevena and my dad.

"Hey," Nevena says. "I'm leaving."

"Hi," I respond. "Did you come over for dinner?" I hang up my coat and tuck my gloves in the pockets. It's late enough that I've missed Mom's strict six p.m. meal time.

They exchange a glance and suppress a smile, which sets off an alarm bell in my head. I'm still a little mad at my parents and the rest of my sisters. Daria hiring a nanny is a big step. So far, all my dad's done is gone quiet, as if he has nothing to say to me that's not harassing me about finishing my degree.

"What?"

"Nothing," they say in unison, looking suspicious.

"Mom will heat your plate up again." Dad juts his chin back toward the kitchen, where my mom's voice filters out. Who is she talking to?

I say goodbye to Nevena and walk with Dad through the living room to the kitchen, hoping I'm not about to get a huge delayed lecture from my parents—or kicked out, though that's unlikely—but a third person sitting at the counter has me stopping in my tracks.

Peter is here.

He's at the counter, next to my mom, eating the stuffed cabbage rolls she made a few nights ago. He looks up when my mom stops talking and sees me. Putting the fork down, he chews quickly and then swallows.

"Hi," he says.

"I'll put your plate in the microwave," Mom says, getting up.

"Mom, I can do it."

"It'll take me two seconds."

Peter turns to face me, wiping his palms on the thigh of his jeans.

"How did you know where to find me?" I ask.

"Your address is at the bottom of your invoices."

The microwave door slams shut. Mom sets the cook time once, then mutters, "No, no, too long," before hitting cancel.

"I was at Heartly today, actually. You should have called."

Mom starts over with the microwave. Finally, it starts, and Mom raises her hands. "I'm going, I'm going."

She and Dad retreat to the front room, where they're going to pretend they aren't listening.

"What are you doing here?"

"I felt terrible with how we left each other in Zurich, and I had to see you again. I wanted to tell you that you don't have to move your business to Zurich. That was dumb, and it was me trying desperately to find a way to see you more."

I step closer, taking the seat my mother abandoned and facing him.

"I do want to see you again. I can come to New York whenever you want because it's worth seeing you again, no matter where it happens."

One of his hands hangs off the edge of the counter, and I take it in mine. "I thought about it a lot, and you were right. I *could* rebuild my business. I'm not saying I want to, but I have to have faith in myself that I can do whatever I want to do—within reason."

Peter flips his hands over and threads his fingers through mine. "You can do whatever you want to. I have enough faith in you for the both of us."

I smile. "I know you do."

"Good." He lifts my hand, pressing the back of it to his lips in a soft kiss. "Kara, will you go out to dinner with me?"

I pretend to think about it. "No."

Peter's face freezes, eyes darting between mine in uncertainty.

The microwave dings. "We're going to eat this food my mom prepared, and you're going to stay till New Year's Eve if you can—" I look at Peter, and he gives me one of his rare grins. "—and you'll spend those three days getting to know *my* family. You know," I shrug casually, "to make sure you're serious about this relationship."

Peter leans in. "I'm sure. But I'll spend time with your family on one condition."

"What's that?" I lean in until our noses brush.

"We get a hotel room so we can be as loud as we want."

EPILOGUE - KARA

ABOUT TEN MONTHS LATER . . .

I'm sitting on the floor of a generic office space, surrounded by boxes and fabric, when my phone dings.

BEA

It's a Christmas miracle.

KARA

Hmm . . . it's October.

BEA

Fine, it's a Halloween miracle.

Ugh, no, that sounds like raising the dead.

CLARA

Get to the miracle.

BEA

We are NOT going to upstate New York for Christmas this year.

I repeat: WE ARE NOT GOING TO THAT PODUNK TOWN AND THAT TERRIBLE CABIN FOR CHRISTMAS.

I laugh. The three of us have been talking a lot about holiday plans lately. Since Christmas and Hanukkah don't overlap this year, Peter and I are hosting both at our new place.

My parents have floated the idea of my sisters celebrating with their in-laws and the two of them coming across the pond for Christmas. And then, of course, Peter's whole family wants to visit for Hanukkah. So it'll be a busy December.

CLARA

Wow, what changed?

BEA

I don't know. But that's not even the best part.

The best part is that Charlie isn't coming.

Apparently, he's got some kind of dust-up with his company, and he's going to be too busy to join us.

CLARA

Woot! That is exciting.

KARA

Bea, remind me what company Charlie works for again?

BEA

He runs his own company that has something to do with virtual reality.

It's not hardware or gaming. It has something to do with sensor input?

I don't know.

His parents brag about him all the time, but they don't understand it either.

I'm almost home from a late night at the office, so I'm going to pop open some sparkling wine to celebrate.

That means your husband is also leaving the office, btw Clara.

Also, Kara, what are you doing up? Isn't it like two am in London?

It is. The windows looking out over the city are dark, the fluorescent lights above me glaringly bright. I could be anywhere in the world with this blah décor and unremarkable view out my window. But I'm in London, where Peter and I moved in together in July.

KARA

Umm . . . working?

Remember Sylvie's video that went viral? About the dress she made? Ever since then, we've been insanely busy. The padded bralette she talked about is our most requested item now.

I'm glad to volunteer my time with a gender-affirming clothing distribution charity, especially while I'm still building my client base in London, but damn. This is a lot of clothes to sort through and package. I thought I'd paid my dues of late nights and grunt work.

CLARA

It's because the products are awesome. And free.

They gotta get out the door somehow.

KARA

Thanks.

> I do like the video consults better, but you are right; these binders aren't going to ship themselves.

BEA

> That would be a trick.

KARA

> Two more packages to go and then bedtime.

CLARA

> When we visit next week, maybe we can help? You know, something to do while Nash and Peter are meeting with the London office.

BEA

> I'll have to see how much Nash needs me, but TOTALLY!

KARA

> Thanks! I appreciate it. Okay, bedtime. See you sooooooon.

My friends go quiet, and I pack up the last of the clothing. I text Peter that I'm on my way home and climb into a rideshare outside of the building.

We drive past the fish and chips shop that Peter and I eat at when he meets me at the charity, the coffee shop where I occasionally buy breakfast if I'm hungry and running late. The buildings are all closed up and dark, like our house is when the driver pulls up on the curb.

I get out with a "thank you" and enter our house as quietly as possible. Twenty minutes later, I'm slipping into bed next to my sleeping boyfriend, gently putting my knee on the bed and easing my weight so as to not disturb him.

When I get flat on my back, I lie still. Peter's breaths are deep and even, and I think I've done it.

Just as I relax, though, a warm arm bands around me. I'm

pulled toward Peter and bounced around as he squirms to get through my hair and plant a kiss on the back of my neck.

"I lieb di," he mutters. It's Swiss-German for "I love you," and he only says it that way when he's half-asleep.

My heart melts for him all over again.

———

The End

AUTHOR'S NOTE

Though I'm half-Jewish on my dad's side, I was not raised in Judaism. My Jewish ancestors were spread throughout Europe, from France to Russia, and I enjoyed exploring rituals and traditions that they practiced. I chose a surname from my family tree for Peter.

Also, Swiss-German language proved to be difficult to translate, as it is a collection of dialects instead of one written language. Thank you to my friends who made spelling suggestions and assured me that it is hard to go wrong when there aren't hard-and-fast rules.

Thank you to my Jewish early readers for their assistance in this story and to my trans sensitivity reader, Maxie. Any errors or fumbles contained within are entirely my fault.

I am not Christian either, but I hope I conveyed the joy I feel with family traditions and, most of all, spending precious time with our loved ones.

ACKNOWLEDGMENTS

I wrote and published Nutcracker with Benefits on a whim. I just wanted to write a Nutcracker retelling, and I didn't expect it to be so popular. I love the warm, gooey feelings that the holidays invoke, no matter which one you're celebrating.

Thank you to Lillian Lark, Sara Whitney, Lainey David, Allie Lasky, and Sister Grimm for reading early versions of this book and making thoughtful suggestions. Thank you also to Maxie Mettler, my sensitivity reader, and Lisa Matsumura, my proofreader.

And as always, a big thank-you to my husband, who encouraged me so much from day one, and my parents, all five of them, who supported this book in one way or another.

ABOUT LIZ ALDEN

Liz Alden is a digital nomad. Most of the time she's on her sailboat, but sometimes she's in Texas. She knows exactly how big the world is—having sailed around it—and exactly how small it is, having bumped into friends worldwide.

She's been a dishwasher, an engineer, a CEO, and occasionally gets paid to write or sail.

The books are inspired by her real-life travel.

Follow Liz:

www.ingramcontent.com/pod-product-compliance
Lightning Source LLC
Chambersburg PA
CBHW030832200726
48285CB00007B/2414